"Okay, Jase," said Derek. "Make it a good one."

I ran at the line, put my foot down so my toes just missed the disqualifying line, and sailed. I knew while still in the air that I was jumping my best jump. I threw myself forward as I landed so I wouldn't ruin it by falling backwards.

I climbed out of the sand as Jeremy, Derek, and Earl cheered. It was definitely a great jump, probably not good enough for meet competition, but great for me.

"Again!" I yelled. "Let me jump again! I want to make certain it wasn't a fluke."

I took off and flew like I had wings. . . .

A Race to the Finish

GAYLE ROPER

Chariot Books™
David C. Cook Publishing Co.

A White Horse Book
Published by Chariot Books™,
an imprint of David C. Cook Publishing Co.
David C. Cook Publishing Co., Elgin, Illinois 60120
David C. Cook Publishing Co., Weston, Ontario

A RACE TO THE FINISH
© 1991 by Gayle Roper

Cover design by Loran Berg
Cover illustration by Paul Turnbaugh
First printing, 1991
Printed in the United States of America
95 94 93 92 91 5 4 3 2 1

Library of Congress Cataloging-in-Publication Data

Roper, Gayle G.
  A race to the finish / Gayle G. Roper
    p. cm.—(A Sports story for boys) (A White horse book)
  Summary: A young track athlete and candidate for
"Mayor for a Day" learns to trust in God when problems
arise.
    ISBN 1-55513-816-0
    [1. Track and field—Fiction. 2. Elections—Fiction.
3. Christian life—Fiction.] I. Title. II. Series.
PZ7.R6788Rac 1991
[Fic]—dc20   90-21160
                                                            CIP
                                                            AC

for the nephews

Chuck	Curt
Carl	Chad
Nate	Tom

A special thanks to Mr. Henry Cordenner, former track coach, North Brandywine Junior High School, Coatesville, Pa.

Thanks also to Laurel Crane, 11; Kelly Roussey, 9; Tommy Roussey, 12; Ryan Junkins, 13; and Todd Junkins, 12, for their help.

1

"Well, Jase McCarver," the giant said to me as he stood blocking the door to the locker room. "You're going out for track?" he sneered.

I tried to ignore both him and his comment, but it was hard. I am an ordinary seventh-grade kid, short still and kind of shy, but Rand is huge and mean. I always feel like a little bump in the ground that an ant could jump over whenever I get too close to his Mt. Everest body. And he knows it.

The truth is Rand Purcell is a jerk. He also happens to be my least favorite person in the world. I know he's got a bad home life and nobody likes him and I should be nice to him. My mother keeps telling me that. But . . .

He leaned real close, sort of hanging over me like a hungry vulture, and said, "I guess if Mr. Andretti lets you run on a day with a strong wind, you might be able to make it around the track once."

He laughed loudly at his dumb joke and let the locker-room door slip shut in my face.

"Come on, Jase." My best friend Mike grabbed me by the arm. "Let's get out of here. Who needs Rand? Who wants to spend spring playing track?"

"Running track," I corrected. "And we do."

"We do?"

"Of course we do."

"I don't know anything about track except you sweat when you run it, and I don't need to know anything more," said Mike who always reminded me of a short Pillsbury Doughboy with glasses. "I hate it already."

"But you told Mr. Andretti you'd be a manager."

"Only because you had my arm twisted behind my back."

"But your word is still your word," I reminded him. "Besides you can't spend your whole life with your nose in some computer magazine."

"I'd like to know why not."

"Mike, Mr. Andretti's expecting you. You can't let him down."

Mike made a monster face at me.

I smiled encouragingly. "Managers don't have to run or sweat, you know. They just manage. All you have to do is stand around and look busy."

"Can you guarantee me that Mr. Andretti won't ask me to run?" Mike was dead serious.

"Did you have to play soccer when you were the soccer manager?" I asked.

"No. But they made me chase the out-of-bounds balls!"

"There are no out-of-bounds balls in track and field," I assured him.

He looked unconvinced, but at least he didn't go home. He went in search of Mr. Andretti, and I went into the locker room to change.

I wasn't sure what to expect from track. I only knew what I had seen on TV. I also knew that I liked to run. I thought I could run fast, but I didn't know if I was fast enough. And I didn't know how the races worked. What if I had to run against a giant like Rand? I shivered. He'd probably sneak over and trip me every chance he got and I'd spend all season digging cinders out of my knees.

But it was track or nothing. I knew it, and so did my good friends Jeremy and Fonz. In spite of all our years in Little League, we weren't very good at baseball, the other spring sport at Keystone Junior High.

When I got outside, I found Fonz and Jeremy, and we waited in the warm April afternoon sun to see what was going to happen. There were lots of other guys in sweats standing around, too. The three of us tried to determine how strong our competition was going to be this season.

Mr. Andretti was standing with Mr. Zindorf, who was the assistant track coach, and they both looked very official with clipboards in their hands. Mike stood with them trying to look important, too. Unfortunately he needed a clipboard and clean glasses to pull it off, and he had neither.

"Line up according to height," ordered Mr. Andretti.

Fonz and I found ourselves near the beginning of the line, Jeremy was somewhere in the middle, and, thank goodness, Rand was at the end, far, far away.

"Count off by six," Mr. Andretti called. "Then each six make your own line, ones in the front, sixes last. Face me."

I was three and Fonz four in the first line. We began doing exercises—stretching, bending, jumping. In fact, for twenty minutes we did everything but run.

"We will be warming up like this every day," Mr. Andretti told us. "If you try to run without a proper warm-up, you will pull a muscle and be out for the rest of the season. Don't try and cheat here. I know it's boring, but you must do it."

The eighth graders looked resigned, but a number of the seventh graders were unhappy. They wanted the fun of running, not the discipline of working out. I bet they wouldn't stick with it.

"Mr. Zindorf will take the seventh graders to the track to work with the starting blocks. Eighth graders, come with me." Mr. Andretti turned and began to jog, the eighth-grade guys following.

Mr. Zindorf held up two pieces of wood joined by a rope. One side of each wood block was cut on an angle.

"Have any of you ever used starting blocks before?" he asked.

None of us had, so he demonstrated how we should crouch over them, feet resting against the angled part. We then had something to push off of when we began to run. He put six sets of blocks on the track and told us to take turns practicing with them.

"On your mark! Get set! Go!" he yelled again and again.

We took off, once, twice, ten times, trying to do what he said.

"Don't straighten up right away, McCarver," he called as I stood up with my first steps. "Rise slowly! Jeremy Barnes, bottom's up and look toward the finish line. Purcell, set with your fingers, not your palms. There's no spring in your palms."

The blocks felt awkward when I used them and I tried not to stand up right away, but it was hard. I tried to set myself correctly, leaning my weight on my fingers with my bottom as high as I could get it.

It wasn't until we finally got to run that I felt I knew what I was doing.

I've liked to run as far back as I can remember. That was one of the reasons I enjoyed soccer so much. There was something about eating up the distance that I found exciting and fun. But I hadn't run much over the winter, and when Mr. Zindorf yelled, "Walk

11

once around," my heaving chest was very relieved.

After practice I was waiting for Dad to pick me up when Mike came out looking most unhappy.

"You lied," he told me.

"What?"

"You said I'd just have to manage, not do any work."

"I said you wouldn't have to run. Did you have to run?"

"No, but I had to carry. I had to bring all the equipment out—the blocks, the shot, the discus. Those things are heavy!"

"Think of the muscles you'll be getting," I said. "Soon you'll look like one of those oily bodybuilders."

"Sure," said Mike. But he wasn't mad anymore. He's a great friend because he doesn't know how to stay angry.

"Hey, Jase," called Rand. He was standing with several of the eighth graders and was bigger than most of them. "Are we waiting for your father?"

I grit my teeth. Every sports season my dad, who is sometimes too nice for my good, drove Rand home. I felt sad that Rand's mother didn't care for him enough to come and get him, and that he had no dad and all that. Still, I hated to put up with him even a moment longer than necessary, especially in my own family car.

"Mike and I are waiting for my father," I said.

Rand laughed. "It's a good thing your dad's a better Christian than you," he said. "At least he likes to help people."

I rolled my eyes. The guy was so insulting! Now Dad would have to take him home or look like some lousy person. And he wasn't a lousy person. In fact, both he and Mom were pretty good as parents go.

I knew they seemed wonderful to Rand and Mike because their own families were so terrible. Somebody told me once that only children get spoiled, but they hadn't met Ms. Purcell or Mr. and Mrs. Viders.

Ms. Purcell, Rand's mom, was an unmarried businesswoman who seemed to be nice to everyone but Rand. She went out with lots of men and left Rand alone most of the time, even years ago when he was little. I've heard her whip Rand with her nasty mouth on a couple of occasions, and it was so bad even I felt sorry for him, though I'd never tell him. He'd just dump on me harder.

Mike lived next door to us, so I knew his family pretty well. They were no great shakes either. He stayed at our house as much as he could because they fought so much. One of them was always walking out on the other, always with screaming and name-calling and throwing things. Mike had a lot more freedom than I did because his parents were too busy hating each other to have much time to love him.

Being loved can be a burden sometimes, but being ignored like Mike and Rand, was horrible all the time.

Dad pulled up and Mike and I climbed in the backseat. Rand walked over to the car slowly, like a puppy who thinks he might get kicked. After all he'd said to me, I was surprised that he hesitated like that. He seemed to be holding his breath.

Maybe he wouldn't be riding with us after all!

"Hop in, Rand," called my father. "We'll be glad to take you home."

Rand started breathing again and climbed in, a big smile on his face.

I looked at Mike and shook my head. Life can be awfully difficult sometimes.

2

"Now tell us all about track," said Mom as we sat down for dinner. "I know you must be enjoying it already."

"Mom, we're talking hard work, not fun!"

"Isn't hard work allowed to be fun?" she asked.

"Not physical work," said Mike who was eating with us. "Physical work is terrible. Mental games are the challenge and the fun."

Mom looked at Mike like she frequently did, as if he were an alien from some weird place. She liked him a lot and often felt sorry for him, but she thought he was strange. And I guess in a nice way, he was.

"What did you do at practice today?" asked my little brother Matty. Matty is two years younger than

I am and has red hair and blue eyes. He doesn't look anything like me, but he's a good kid. "Did you run much? I bet you had fun."

"We worked, Matty," I said. "We worked hard."

And practice continued to be hard work. As I had expected, by the end of the first week, a number of seventh graders dropped out because they couldn't stand the discipline. All they wanted was glory, but they weren't willing to sweat for it. That was one problem with TV sports, my father always said. We saw only the praise and popularity, not the agony and hard work that got the athletes to that point of excellence.

Mr. Andretti and Mr. Zindorf kept elaborate records on each of us, timing us again and again, trying us in different events to see where we did the best. I seemed to do well at the shorter distances, but as my wind improved, so did my distance running. I had no idea where I'd end up.

I found I liked practicing for relays.

"You will receive the baton in your left hand," Mr. Zindorf said. "Then you will transfer it to your right hand as you run. You must be ready to pass it to the next man with your right hand to his left. That way you won't step on his heels as you come up behind him. You'll be off to his left side."

"All I can say," yelled Fonz as he and I fumbled the baton on a practice run, "is that it looks a lot easier on TV."

"Again!" yelled Mr. Zindorf. "Jase and Fonz, do it again. And again. Do it until you do it five times in a row without flubbing the baton pass."

One of the unexpected and happy things about junior high track was that it was organized by the weight of the participants, sort of like wrestling, so Rand was rarely near me. I ran and I passed the baton and I practiced on the starting blocks in peace and quiet. It was great.

One Thursday a couple of weeks into the season, Mr. Andretti looked at us. It was a cool, sunny April day, the kind that makes me feel bouncy.

"You've got the makings of a great team," he told us. "I know you eighth graders are a talented bunch because you proved it last year. And it looks like we have an exceptional group of seventh graders." He smiled. "It's going to be a fine year."

We all smiled back at him. Even though we knew it was the coach's job to say stuff like that, it still made us feel good.

"Today we'll begin working on the field events. Those of you who are interested in discus, shot, high jump or long jump come with me. The rest of you go with Mr. Zindorf."

I followed Mr. Andretti. I was interested in the long jump. I didn't know if I was big enough, but I wanted to try. After all, I didn't plan to be a little guy all my life.

Jeremy wanted to try long jump, too, and so did a couple of eighth graders I didn't know. Mr. Andretti sent us to the jump pit on the field.

"Derek, you're in charge," he told the biggest kid.

He pointed to Jeremy and me. "Show these guys what to do, and I'll be along as soon as I can."

We practiced jumping, trying always to throw our bodies forward when we landed. The distance of each jump was based on the point you touched closest to the takeoff. If you lost your balance and fell backwards, measurement went to your seat mark or your hand mark instead of to where your feet landed.

I found out quickly that Jeremy was going to be a good jumper, that Derek and his pal Earl were good, and that I would need a lot of work. I kept stepping on the foul line at takeoff or falling backwards when I landed or jumping about two whole big inches. My size was against me.

"Spread your knees when you land," said Derek. "Lean forward between them. Look where you're going."

I tried to do all he told me, and I was worse than ever.

"Maybe you ought to try hurdles if you want to jump," suggested Derek kindly.

"No," I said. "I don't want to run at something full speed and have to jump over it. I'll just keep working here."

Once when Derek and Earl were jumping, I took time to look around. Not too far from us, Mr. Andretti was working with Rand and a couple of other big guys on how to throw the shot.

Rand had the shot cradled in his right hand, resting it on his shoulder. Mr. Andretti demonstrated a whirling turn and mimed letting go. Rand nodded his head in understanding. The shot looked so natural in his gigantic palm that I knew he was going to be good. I was glad for the team, but I was not glad for me. He'd be too happy bragging, especially when he learned how sad I was at the long jump. I sighed.

"Hey, Mike!" yelled Mr. Andretti. "Go down there and catch the shot for me." He pointed down the field.

Mike looked pained but he dutifully ran to the place indicated.

Rand spun around just like Mr. Andretti had shown him and threw the shot as hard as he could. The heavy metal ball flew through the air a very long distance. I glanced at Rand who was smirking with pleasure and at Mr. Andretti who looked like he'd been handed an unexpected present.

I kicked the ground, not enough for anyone to notice, just enough to let out some of my frustration. Rand was good indeed.

Suddenly Mr. Andretti began shouting and waving his hands and yelling, "No!"

I looked, and there was Mike, positioning himself under the shot to catch it, just like you'd do with a baseball. The goof! He was going to get hurt or maybe even killed!

Mr. Andretti began running and I began running and everybody began shouting, "No! No! Get away! Get away!"

All the noise broke Mike's concentration on the metal ball rapidly falling toward him. He took a step backwards and looked around for the problem everyone was yelling about. While he looked, the shot thudded harmlessly to the ground in front of him. It made a small dent in the turf.

"But you said I should go catch the thing," Mike defended himself when he realized he had been the cause for all the excitement.

"I didn't mean catch it like you'd catch a baseball!" roared Mr. Andretti. "That thing could have broken your hand or knocked you out!"

"How am I supposed to know that?" Mike answered. "I'm only the manager!" He stalked off toward the school while Mr. Andretti and Mr. Zindorf did their best to curb the laughter of the team. It was hard going for them because, now that the danger was over, they were laughing, too.

"I'm going back to my computer magazines," said Mike on the way home. "They never fall on me, they never yell at me, they never make me feel like an idiot, and they never make me sweat!"

"You can't quit," I said.

"Jase is right," said Rand from the front seat beside my father. "You can't quit."

I blinked. Rand and I were actually agreeing on something. It was scary.

Rand continued, "You can't quit because I need you around for laughs!" And he began to laugh like something really funny had just happened.

I grabbed Mike's arm and whispered, "You can't leave me alone with him!"

Mike looked pained and undecided.

"Mike, I agree with Jase and Rand," said Dad. "You shouldn't quit. It's not that long a season, for one thing. For another and more important thing, Mr. Andretti is counting on you."

"Yeah, yeah," muttered Mike. But the crisis was over. He'd stay. I could tell by his voice. I flopped back on the seat and smiled out the window.

3

Sunday night in the beginning of May the phone rang. It was Tobi Jo Joiner, one of the girls in my homeroom, and she wanted to talk to me. I couldn't imagine why.

"Wait 'til I tell Mary Ellen," said Mike who, as usual, was at our house. "She's got competition."

"Get lost, Mike," I snarled, then smiled into the phone and tried not to sound nervous. "What can I do for you, Tobi Jo?"

"I'm having a big party not this Friday but next, Jase, and I'd like you to come. It's for my thirteenth birthday." She sounded all sparkly. She had real short, curly hair. I could just see her curls going SPROING with her excitement. "Jeremy and Fonz and Mary

Ellen and Sally and Rand and a whole bunch of kids are coming."

"Sounds like fun," I said. Except for Rand, of course. "Thanks."

"Sounds like fun," said Mom when I told her. "I know you'll have a wonderful time. Tobi Jo is a nice girl."

I shrugged. Tobi Jo was nice enough, but the girl I really liked was Mary Ellen Lafferty. Not that she knew it. I was too scared to do anything but worship her from afar.

Every day on the bus trip to school, I watched Mary Ellen appear like magic as she climbed the steps into the bus. First her shiny gold hair, then her smiling face, then the rest of her. I liked it when she wore bright blue because it made her eyes bluer. She sat beside Tobi Jo every day, and I dreamed that one day she'd sit by me.

"Dream on," Mike told me all the time. "But don't hold your breath until your dream comes true. You won't do me any good as a friend if you're dead of heartbreak."

Sally was Mary Ellen's other good friend. Sally went to my church, and sometimes she brought Mary Ellen along for the youth group socials. On those occasions life could hardly be better.

It wasn't until I was ready to fall asleep the night of the invitation that I realized that Mike wasn't among Tobi Jo's invitees. And neither, I found out the next day, was fuzzy old Judy Post.

Judy was one of those people who looked like a bomb went off in their bedroom while they were getting dressed, and there wasn't time to undo its damage. Her hair either stuck out weirdly or hung in her eyes, and her clothes looked like she had pulled them out of the dirty clothes hamper instead of the closet. She always looked scared and sounded scared. She was one of the smartest girls I knew, almost as smart as Mary Ellen, and you'd think she'd be able to learn how to look nice. She used to like me, but she didn't anymore, thank goodness.

We were in morning homeroom when Tobi Jo began talking about the plans for her party.

"I'm having a disc jockey," she bubbled. "My father says I only become a teenager once, so let's have the biggest blast we can."

There were lots of impressed faces around Tobi Jo. No one had ever had a disc jockey at any other party.

"And my mom is having a caterer do the food, so don't you guys eat before you come."

"We won't. Don't worry," everyone assured her. "What are we eating?"

"Do you think I'd tell you and ruin the surprise?" Tobi Jo giggled and shook her head. Her curls went SPROING! "You have to come to find out. And you have to get dressed up to come."

"Is the whole class coming?" asked Jeremy.

"Oh, no," said Tobi Jo. "Just those I invited." She leaned toward Jeremy and lowered her voice. "And they know who they are."

I could see Judy Post just over Tobi Jo's shoulder. She had been listening to the details of the party as keenly as the rest of us. But when Tobi Jo said that not everyone was invited and Judy realized she was one who wasn't, she sat back in her seat and sort of collapsed inward. It was like watching a balloon lose its air.

Suddenly Judy became very involved in looking for a paper in her notebook. She glanced quickly at Tobi Jo out of the corner of her eye, then reached up and wiped a tear from her cheek.

A tear! I couldn't believe it! Judy was crying about not going to Tobi Jo's party!

I sat back and thought. Was it that bad not to be included? I looked at Mike. He was avoiding looking at Tobi Jo and the kids just as hard as Judy was. His ears were red, like they always got when he was upset. He wasn't about to cry, but he was obviously hurt, too.

Suddenly I felt mad on behalf of Tobi Jo's party. What was the matter with having a party? And what was the matter with asking the people you wanted? It wasn't my fault that I got asked and Mike didn't. It wasn't my fault that Tobi Jo talked too much. It wasn't my fault that nothing worked out right for Judy or that she and Mike were nerds. I was invited and I was going and I would have a good time!

4

I ran out to the field for the first official track meet of the season with huge butterflies in my stomach. It was a nasty, cold May Monday, and I shivered in my sweats, partly from the weather, partly from excitement, and partly from nervousness, though I tried not to let it show. I watched the guys from Lyme Junior High School while we warmed up. I tried to make myself think they were all wimps.

Mr. Andretti had a list of all the events and who was participating in what. Each of us was allowed to be in three events, and my three were the 100-meter dash (85 pounds and under), the 400-meter relay (85 pounds and under), and the 800-meter relay (100 pounds and under).

Fonz was chosen for the same events, though running on a different 800-meter team than I was. Jeremy was in the 100-meter dash (100 pounds and under), the long jump, and he was second runner to my first on my 800-meter relay team.

Mom and Matty were shivering in the stands, and I waved to them. My family came to everything I was in, and we went to all Matty's things, too. I know Dad liked coming to our sports things much more than to my school band concerts, but he even came to the concerts.

This show of family support both pleased me and embarrassed me, mostly because my mom yelled too loudly.

"Come on, Jase! I know you can do it!" or "That's the way, Jase! I knew you could do it!" echoed sharply wherever she was. Nobody ever had a better fan, but nobody ever had a noisier one either.

Mary Ellen, Sally, and Tobi Jo were in the stands, too, yelling along with the cheerleaders. Sitting by herself in one corner looking lost and forlorn was Judy Post.

When I set myself on the blocks for my first race, I kept saying over and over, "Stand up slowly! Stand up slowly!"

"On your mark! Get set!" yelled the official.

I put my seat up like Mr. Zindorf had taught us and looked at the finish tape. What if I tripped and fell? What if, when I fell, I took someone down with me? My heart was so loud in my ears, I was afraid I wouldn't hear the starter's shot.

I needn't have worried. The BANG! sounded, and I took off. I didn't stand straight up, but I didn't stay crouched long enough either.

The surprising thing was that I felt like I was running in slow motion. My feet were so heavy I could hardly move them. I'd never had that experience running before. I loved to run. I should be flying. Instead the tape looked so far away! I knew I'd never get there.

Run, you dummy, I shouted at myself. *Run!*

Suddenly the finish line was behind me and the race was over. Fonz grabbed me and jumped up and down, up and down.

"You were second and I was third," he yelled over and over.

I was? How could that be? I had hardly moved!

"You guys looked great!" yelled Jeremy as he lined up for his race. "Great!"

"Nice going," called Mr. Zindorf.

When I got Fonz to calm down, I found out that the winner of our race was a little eighth grader from Lyme. I wondered how many times eighth graders beat seventh graders. Did that year of experience make a big difference?

We pulled on our sweats and watched Jeremy run his dash. He came in third behind two kids from Lyme.

"Eighth graders?" I asked.

"One is; one isn't," I was told.

I could see right away that I couldn't hide behind

the excuse of "eighth grader" whenever I lost. I'd have to be more careful not to use such an easy defense.

The 115-pound kids ran and Derek won. He was an eighth grader. But it was seventh-grade Rand speeding down the track in the open-class dash that was the most exciting. He was step for step with a big kid from Lyme, but he leaned into the tape first and won. How great for us that he was so good; how bad for Rand's big head.

I had fun at my first track meet. There was always something going on, though they only ran one event at a time. The field events were interesting to watch, and Derek took a first and Earl a third in the long jump. Rand threw the shot like he'd been doing it all his life, reaching thirty-five feet, a very good distance for anyone, eighth grade or seventh grade.

My 400-meter relay team finished third and my 800-meter relay team took first. I was excited to do so well, but Rand did better. Besides his first in the dash, he took second in the shot and his relay team was first.

We beat Lyme by 10 points.

Mr. Andretti was excited. "It's going to be a great year," he said to anyone who would listen. When there was no one around, he said it to himself as he rubbed his hands together.

Mr. Andretti was our social studies teacher as well as our track coach. I liked his class because he was an interesting person for a teacher. In fact, sometimes he got just as excited about history as he got about track. I don't understand it myself, but it's true.

It was the day after the track meet that he got all excited in class again, and this time I slowly got excited, too.

"We're going to begin a project today that will take a couple of weeks to finish, but I think you'll like it," he said to our class that morning. "For the fifteenth year we're going to select a Mayor for a Day."

He was standing at the front of the room with a handful of papers.

"I have here petitions that I will distribute to anyone interested in running for Mayor for a Day. The three people in the seventh grade who collect the most signatures will campaign against each other for everyone else's vote. The winner of the election will become Mayor for a Day."

I admit I wasn't moved at first by the idea of the election. What could a seventh-grade kid do as Mayor for a Day except have to wear a suit and act not bored? He certainly wouldn't be allowed to make a law or anything.

"The winner of the election gets to be the Mayor of Radley Park on the Fourth of July," said Mr. Andretti. "That means that the winner rides in the Fourth of July parade with Mayor Armitage and gets a special seat for himself or herself and a guest at all the festivities including the fireworks."

Suddenly being Mayor for a Day sounded much better. I didn't have to like politics to ride in an open convertible in a parade. Mayors always rode in open convertibles, didn't they? I had never heard of Mayor Armitage of Radley Park, but I wouldn't tell him that as we sat and smiled at the cheering crowds together and oohed and aahed at the fireworks.

I looked around the room for possible candidates other than me. I didn't see anyone who struck me as a sure winner. I looked at the papers in Mr. Andretti's hand. Again I imagined myself riding through town, smiling and waving to the crowds.

I think Mr. Andretti said some more things, but I wasn't listening. I put my hands under my desk and waved by swiveling my wrist just like Princess Diana did it. I was a natural.

"Remember, you can only sign one petition," Mr. Andretti was telling the class when I started listening again. "Take your time about signing a petition. You want to be certain you are supporting someone you feel comfortable with. The petition gathering begins tomorrow morning when you arrive at school, not a minute sooner, not even on the bus. You can disqualify yourself by jumping the gun. All of the petitions must be handed in Friday morning. That's three days from now, in case you can't count very well."

I was the first in line to get a petition. I thought more kids would be interested, but only five of us took one. Mary Ellen was behind me, and so were Jeremy and Fonz and then fuzzy old Judy Post. Of course there were other social studies sections, and kids from those classes would compete, too.

"We, the undersigned, support the candidacy of _____ for the office of Mayor for a Day in the town of Radley Park, Pa."

I rested my petition on my desk and filled in the blank with JASON McCARVER in large letters— just like John Hancock. Then I signed my name next to number one.

There were about 200 of us in the whole seventh grade. If I wanted to be one of the three candidates, I'd need at least a third of the kids or sixty-five to seventy to sign for me.

I looked at my signature with satisfaction. Now I only needed sixty-four others.

When I told the family about the election at dinner, Dad asked, "How did the seventh grade get to have the Mayor for a Day? I've seen these kids in the parade in the past, and I always wondered where they found so many short twelfth graders."

"I think the seniors have elections, too," I said. "But they do it in the fall and only get to run the town for a day. We get to be in the parade. Our program started when Mr. Andretti, who teaches social studies, had a relative who was mayor."

"That would be his father," said Dad. "I remember when Mark Andretti was mayor as long as the local laws allowed."

"What is he now?" I asked. "Dogcatcher?"

"No, Jason. In this city a person can only serve three terms as mayor. Now he is the representative serving our district in the State House of Representatives in Harrisburg," Dad said.

I was impressed. Maybe that Mr. Andretti would come visit my Mr. Andretti for the holiday and ride in the convertible with me, too. I could handle that.

"My Mr. Andretti probably gives each new mayor some line about teaching us future citizens and voters how the democratic process works," I said. "You know, America in action and all that stuff." I shrugged. "I don't care why they still do it; I'm just glad they do."

"So you think it's going to be you riding with Mayor Armitage in the Fourth of July parade?" Dad asked.

"Why not?" I asked. "It's better than walking the whole way with my Little League team or my Cub Scout troop like I used to."

"I'm going to be in the parade with my Little League team," said Matty. "The Phillies. We're the Phillies."

I looked at his new baseball cap, still clean in places. "I was on the Phillies once," I said. "We lost a lot. Just don't wear your spikes in the parade. I did one year and my feet have never been the same. Wear real sneakers."

5

I was pulling on my sweats when Jeremy and Fonz ran up to my gym locker.

"Guess who's running for Mayor for a Day?" Fonz said. "Besides us, I mean."

"Rand!" Jeremy answered before I could even think of a name.

"Rand?" I couldn't believe it. Talk about dumb politicians.

"And that big guy Preston's helping him," said Jeremy.

"What are they going to do? Beat up anyone who won't vote for them?" I asked.

"I think we should all get together behind one person who has a good chance of beating him instead of competing against each other," said Fonz, whose real name is Alphonso, but you'd better never call him that name. He was about my size—small—but he'd attack anyone over his name.

"Sort of like united-we-stand, divided-we-fall," said Jeremy.

"And we think you have the best chance of beating Rand," said Fonz.

"Me?" I tried to look honored, but I was so pleased it was hard. I probably just looked stupid. "Me?"

"Yeah." They nodded. "We'll give you all our signatures and help you get more."

"Me?" I could see those fireworks already.

"Here's to the winner and next Mayor for a Day, Jason McCarver!" yelled Jeremy, shouting my name really loudly. Fonz joined in the cheer. I was standing there grinning when a long shadow fell across the alcove of lockers we were in.

We looked up to see Rand Purcell towering over us, trapping us in our little cubbyhole with his legs astride and his hands resting on the tops of the lockers. I couldn't even reach the tops of the lockers, let alone rest my palms on them like he was doing. He was like an evil giant and we were Jacks with no beanstalk to escape down. I hated the way he made my stomach go flip-flop.

"Mayor for a Day Jason McCarver?" he sneered. "Don't you just wish! Hey, Preston, this little kid thinks he's going to beat me! Can you believe it?"

Snickering nastily the two went out the door.

Jeremy, Fonz, and I looked at each other.

"We can do it," said Jeremy hesitantly.

"Sure we can," said Fonz with a little more enthusiasm.

"We've got to," I said firmly, hoping it would be true. "We can't let him win! We'll just have to work really hard."

And we did. Mike, Jeremy, Fonz, and I walked around the lunchroom as well as all the homerooms, asking for signatures. And we did well. I felt very hopeful.

On the day the petitions were supposed to be handed in, a hand tapped me hesitantly on the shoulder as I sat on the school bus. I turned around to find Judy Post looking timidly at me.

"Jase," she said, "would you sign my petition?"

She stuck a shaggy, very wrinkled piece of paper under my nose. I thought it very interesting that Judy and her paper looked so much alike.

"I'm sorry, Judy. I can't." I noticed she only had about five signatures. "I already signed one, and that's all you can sign."

"I guess I waited too long to get started," she said. "I just thought it would be fun to be in an election."

"The petitions have to be turned in this morning, you know." I reached in my history book and pulled out mine. I held it out toward Judy. It fell open and all the sixty-three signatures showed.

Judy looked at it sadly, then said, "I shouldn't have even tried. I'd never win." She sat back in her seat and looked as if she wanted to cry.

But she was right. She shouldn't have tried. I could have told her that. Judy might be a brain, but being a brain didn't get you nominated for Mayor for a Day. Getting the most signatures did, and no one was going to waste his signature on Judy.

I looked at her again, then carefully refolded my petition and put it back in my history book. I wanted to keep it safe until I turned it and its sixty-three signatures in to Mr. Andretti on my way to homeroom.

"I'll let you know the results before school's over," Mr. Andretti said to our class. "I know the Fourth of July is still far away, but we need to finish this election before we get into reviewing for finals and all the other end-of-the-year things. Besides, you guys are itchy enough in June without an election to make you worse." He grinned when he said it so we wouldn't be offended, and we smiled back. He was right.

I was edgy all day, wondering if I would be one of the candidates. The note with the answer came fifteen minutes before school ended.

"Jason McCarver and Mary Ellen Lafferty, Mr. Andretti has asked to see you," said Mrs. Stevens, my English teacher. We were discussing *Light in the Forest* which I had finished reading the day it got handed out, even though we weren't supposed to read ahead. The what-did-the-writer-mean discussions like we were having always got me in trouble. I never knew what the writers meant, only what they wrote.

I was delighted to go to Mr. Andretti's room.

Mary Ellen and I walked down the hall together. I kept wishing I could think of something witty to say to her, but as usual when I was around her, my brain was in neutral and my tongue in park.

"I guess this is about the petitions," she said. "Do you think maybe we're going to get to run for Mayor for a Day?"

"Who knows?" I said cleverly.

We walked into Mr. Andretti's empty room and sat in the seats right before his desk. Coaches often have their last period free so they can go to games or meets without messing a class up.

"I've tallied all the petitions," Mr. Andretti said, "and I'm pleased to tell you that you two have won the right to campaign for the Mayor for a Day honor. There is another candidate, but he hasn't arrived yet."

I was grinning; I could feel it. I probably looked a lot like a short human version of a smiley face sticker. I peeked at Mary Ellen. She was smiling, too.

I can beat her, I thought. She's a girl. Sure, she's the prettiest, nicest, smartest girl in the whole seventh grade, but girls hardly ever get to be Mayor for a Day—or mayor, for that matter.

"Ah," said Mr. Andretti, "here comes our third candidate now."

"Hi, Beautiful," the newcomer said to Mary Ellen. "Hi, Little Jase," he said to me.

I felt my smile shatter like a glass that hit a concrete floor. I turned and looked at the third candidate.

It was my archenemy, Rand Purcell.

"Campaigning begins Monday," Mr. Andretti said to the three of us. "That way you'll have the weekend to plan your campaign. Ask your friends to help you; the more people involved, the better. Good luck to each of you." He stood and shook our hands.

Mike and Jeremy and Fonz were very excited I had won the nomination.

"Pooling our resources worked," said Jeremy. "Now we concentrate on beating Purcell."

"And Lafferty," I said with a grin.

The guys grinned back. "Right. And Lafferty," they said.

The four of us spent Sunday afternoon at my house making signs for the election.

JASE SETS THE PACE was their favorite.

ELECT MAYOR McCARVER was the poster I liked. It sounded good.

Mom helped, taking a huge bunch of name tags with sticky backs and writing JASE SETS THE PACE in red with a blue swirl through the letters. We each peeled the back off a tag and clapped it to our shirts. Mike began to sing "Happy Days Are Here Again." At least that's what he said he was singing. Mike is not musical.

Dad and Matty took black, precut, sticky letters and made a big sign that read GOOD THINGS COME IN SMALL PACKAGES: VOTE McCAR-

VER FOR MAYOR. They pasted pictures of presents they had cut out of Mom's magazines all over the poster.

When we had a great stack of posters and badges, we took a break. Mom fed us her fantastic brownies topped with ice cream.

"I just know you're going to do well, Jase," she said. "I just know it."

"You're my mom, Mom, so you can't say anything different." I grabbed the last brownie when she wasn't looking. "But thanks. And thanks, all of you, for your help. If I'm elected, I promise that I'll give you the day of the parade as a holiday."

It was Matty's balled napkin that hit me first. The others followed in short order, and we had a great napkin fight. When I grabbed an ice cube and went after Fonz, Mom yelled, "Not in my house!" and made us quit.

Jeremy and Fonz went with Mike and me to youth group that evening. They never said much about what they thought of church, and I didn't ask. I was just glad they came with me sometimes. When Pastor Tony announced a miniature golf and ice-cream sundae night in two weeks, they signed up along with Mike and me.

That night Pastor Tony talked about how confusing life can become sometimes.

"Things often don't go as we wish," he said. "That doesn't mean the Lord isn't with us. It just means things don't always go the way we want them to go.

What becomes very important is the way we react when things don't go the way we want."

"Boy, do I know what Pastor Tony means," said Mike on the way home. Mike hadn't been coming to youth group all that long, and he got very excited about all the new-to-him things he heard. I didn't like to admit it, but since Mike thought everything was so interesting at church, I'd started to listen a little better myself.

He leaned over the back of the front seat to talk with Mom and Dad. "Nothing ever seems to go the way *I* wish it would. I mean, look at last Thursday and how stupid I was at practice with the shot. Everybody was laughing at me like I was dumb."

"You were, Mike, old man," said Fonz. "But you were great."

Mike snorted. "The only thing I thought I had going for me was my brains. Now people think I haven't even got them."

"Don't let that episode get you down," said Dad. "We all do things we'd rather no one knew about. It's part of living. Why, just last Tuesday at work . . ."

"Hal," interrupted Mom gently, "Mike understands your point. I don't think you need to tell us about last Tuesday."

"I do understand, Mrs. McCarver," said Mike. "And you're right, Mr. McCarver. We all do stupid things, and they upset us for a while. Then we get over them. I know the shot thing will stop embarrassing me soon. I'm just not there yet. But what about when things don't go right in really important areas? Look at my parents and how they fight so much."

I always felt terrible when Mike talked about his mother and father. First, I couldn't imagine living with people like that. Second, I never knew what to say.

"Did I tell you that my mother punched my father in the chest Friday?" Mike asked. "Right on his fourth shirt button. Knocked the air right out of him. I've never seen them hit each other before. They've thrown things and yelled things and stuff like that, but they have never hit each other. Dad was so surprised that he couldn't move. She was out of the house and gone before he got his breath back."

"She isn't gone for good, is she?" Mom asked. Sympathy flowed from her in waves, and Mike liked it.

"I don't think so. She usually comes back Sunday night if she runs out over the weekend, so I guess she'll come back tonight." Mike shrugged. "I have no idea what revenge Dad has planned. I just know there'll be something and it won't be pretty."

Mom looked at Mike with tears in her eyes. I bet she cared more about him than his own mom did.

"Would you like to spend the night at our house?" she asked. "I know Jase would be happy if you did."

My mom always says she knows what I would like, and this time she was actually right. I'd be happy for Mike's company.

"Could I?" asked Mike. Suddenly he gave a big, relieved sigh. "See? Things don't go the way I want, but the Lord is still with me."

Dad took Mike and me to school early the next day so we could hang my posters and be ready to give out the badges when the buses rolled in.

"Stick them on a book cover or on your shirt or blouse," we told all the kids. When Fonz and Jeremy got there, they helped us. By homeroom, half of the badges were gone. We had decided to give out half today in a big splash for the official start of campaigning and hand the rest out slowly over the next two weeks.

Mary Ellen had the same opening strategy that I did. A poster shouting MARY ELLEN FOR MAYOR or WE'RE ALL YELLIN'—VOTE FOR MARY ELLEN hung on every bulletin board that JASE SETS THE PACE did. She even got the janitor to bring out his ladder and hang a huge sign that she and the girls unrolled. WE'RE ALL YELLIN'—VOTE FOR MARY ELLEN in red, white, and blue stretched across the main hall. It even had red, white, and blue fringe hanging from it. And as if that wasn't enough, she and Tobi Jo and Sally were handing out little bows made of real skinny red, white, and blue ribbon. It must have taken forever to tie them, and every bow had a baby safety pin attached. Only girls would do something that finicky.

Most kids took both my badge and Mary Ellen's bows.

Rand had nothing to hand out or hang up.

43

6

Our track season was really picking up. Everything was going well. We kept getting better and better. We beat Claymont on Tuesday and Marlboro on Thursday.

"Keep up the good work, men," Mr. Andretti would rub his hands together and say. "By the end of the season and the Brandywine Invitational, we'll be unbeatable." He was always trying to encourage us.

The Brandywine Invitational was a huge meet with about thirty junior high schools participating. Keystone sent their team every year, and I knew we had a chance of winning. We were on a roll. Things were going great!

I wish I could say the same for other areas of my life. Friday came and proved to be a disastrous day. Absolutely everything went wrong!

I arrived at school to find a huge poster that said ERASE JASE hanging in the main hall. Attached to it was one of my JASE SETS THE PACE posters made with felt markers. Someone had taken water to it, melting or "erasing" most of JASE SETS THE PACE. A number of the kids thought it was a clever poster, but then it wasn't them being erased. I could almost feel the water melting me.

"Don't let it get you," said Mike. "That's what they want."

I knew that, but I felt weird anyway.

I tore the poster down and ripped it up. I saw Rand watching me as I tossed it in the wastebasket. I had never seen a bigger smirk.

"Oh, Jase!" It was Mary Ellen, looking distressed. "I think it was terrible to do that to your poster. I hope you don't think I did it!"

"Never," I said firmly. I knew who was guilty. "Thanks for caring, though."

"Oh, I do," she said and my heart started pounding with hope. "I would hate to see anything mess up the election. I'm looking forward to riding in the parade."

And with a bright smile, she ran off after Tobi Jo and Sally. So much for romance.

Mr. Andretti was unhappy about the poster and talked to each class about negative compaigning and

45

what he called "underhanded and cruel tactics."

"We do not hold these elections to allow opportunity for one person to personally attack another. If anything else like this happens, I'll cancel the whole election. And if I find out who's guilty. . . ."

He stared at us until even I squirmed.

While I was still trying not to feel upset about the poster, I got a big and unpleasant surprise in band, where I play first-chair trumpet. I'm probably one of the few seventh graders who actually liked band. I think playing my horn is as much fun as running, something none of the other guys understood. Band was one place where I felt confident, at least until practice Friday.

"Jase," said Mr. Keefer, the band director, at the close of practice, "I'm having a hard time making up my mind about who should have the trumpet solo in the spring concert."

I stared at Mr. Keefer. What was to decide? I was first chair. I'd had the solo at Christmas. Surely I should have the solo in the spring concert, too.

"You and Heidi will have to audition."

Heidi! Heidi was in eighth grade, but she played second-chair trumpet. I'd beaten her back in September. That's why she was second and I was first.

"Heidi has improved quite a bit," Mr. Keefer said. "I want to give her a chance."

I looked across the room at Heidi. She was busy putting on this awful pinky-blue lipstick that made her look like she were freezing to death. I never could

46

figure out how someone who spent half her life putting on ugly lipsticks could play such a good trumpet.

In fact, I could never figure out why someone would want to wear lipstick, period. Most of the girls didn't, or if they did, it was very light. But Heidi loved it, the thicker, the better. Maybe she thought it tasted good.

"You've been very good for Heidi," Mr. Keefer told me. "When she was playing with kids who really weren't interested, she didn't apply herself. But when you came along, you challenged her. And she's taken up the challenge. She is much better now than she was in September. Certainly you've noticed the difference."

I nodded. Heidi was doing a lot better. I liked sitting next to her because we'd see who could get a passage right the fastest. Sometimes I won; sometimes she won. But I hadn't meant for her to take my place!

The third blow of the day came in a short meeting of us mayoral candidates with Mr. Andretti.

"Speeches are to be given next Friday," Mr. Andretti told us. "They needn't be long or complicated. In fact, it would probably be better if they weren't."

Speeches?

"All the seventh grade will come to the auditorium first thing next Friday morning to hear you," Mr. Andretti said.

All the seventh grade? Auditorium?

"Keep it short and punchy. It'll help undecided

47

people to make up their minds who to vote for."

Short and punchy? Undecided people?

"I'd like to see the first draft of your speech Wednesday after school."

First draft?

I looked at Mary Ellen and Rand, expecting to see them standing with their mouths hanging open, just like me. But they nodded their heads like they knew exactly what Mr. Andretti was talking about. Obviously I had missed something fairly important somewhere along the line.

I hung back when we were dismissed. If Rand made my stomach do flip-flops, the idea of standing up in front of the whole seventh grade made it shrivel up and die.

"Mr. Andretti," I said, "when did you say we had to give speeches?"

"Next Friday," he said.

"No, I mean when did you first say that each candidate had to give one?"

He shook his head. "I don't remember. Probably when I told your class about the whole program." He looked at me with concern. "Don't you think you can handle it?"

"Oh, I'll be fine," I lied. "No problem at all!" I left the room in a daze. Somehow in the glory of the parade and the cheers, I had missed the agony of the speech.

I put my terrible day from my mind at track practice. I followed the warm-up leaders carefully. I concentrated on rising slowly from the blocks. I stared unflinchingly at the finish line as I sprinted. I worked hard at relay practice, receiving the baton carefully, passing it precisely. At long jump practice, I watched Derek and Earl and Jeremy as they jumped, instead of looking all around like I usually did.

When it was my turn to jump, I determined to do the best I'd ever done.

"Okay, Jase," said Derek. "Make it a good one."

I ran at the line, put my foot down so my toes just missed the disqualifying line, and sailed. I knew while I was still in the air that I was jumping my best jump. I threw myself forward as I landed so I wouldn't ruin it by falling backwards.

I climbed out of the sand as the guys cheered. It was definitely a great jump, probably not good enough for meet competition, but great for me.

"Again!" I yelled. "Let me jump again! I want to make certain it wasn't a fluke."

I took off without disqualifying myself. I flew like I had wings. I threw myself forward.

Unfortunately, I forgot to spread my knees and I threw my face right into my left knee. Actually I hit just to the left of the top of my nose, in the inside of the eye socket.

Stars danced before me and blood gushed from my nose. It seemed very important to get out of the pit so I wouldn't get the sand all red, but my knees wouldn't hold me. I could hear Derek screaming for Mr. Andretti.

They made Mike run for the first-aid kit, and then for a couple of towels from the lost and found box to mop up the blood. They made me sit with my knees bent, leaning forward so the blood dripped onto the ground and not down my throat. They made me hold one of those packs of chemical ice over the bridge of my nose. When the red flood lessened, they made me lie down on the grass. They told me I wasn't going to die.

After a while when the pain lessened, I thought about believing them.

7

At about the time I had planned to leave for Tobi Jo's party, I was leaving the hospital's emergency room with my father and Mike.

"Nothing's broken," the doctor assured us. "Keep ice on it for a couple of days to keep the swelling down. And expect a wingding of a shiner."

I climbed into the car and carefully felt my nose. It was tender and sore but inside I felt even worse. I felt like a first-class, triple-A idiot to have smashed my face so stupidly and to have caused such a fuss.

"Now you know how I felt when I tried to catch the shot," said Mike.

"But you didn't get popped in the nose," I mumbled.

"Only thoroughly embarrassed, which hurts a lot more, as you well know." He grinned. "It'll go away in time. I only feel dumb half the time now."

Sure. In twenty or thirty years I'd probably be able to look back on today without flinching. I went to bed early and stared at the ceiling. The only slightly bright spot in my otherwise very dark day was the fact that Mary Ellen hadn't seen me knock myself silly.

What, I wondered as I drifted off to sleep, do voters think of candidates with swollen noses and black eyes? Was there such a thing as a sympathy vote? Or a klutz backlash?

Jeremy and Fonz biked over to visit me Saturday.

"Just wanted to see if you were alive," Jeremy said.

"I am," I said. "Now tell me about the party."

Fonz and Jeremy looked at each other.

"Well," began Fonz, "I guess it was fine."

"You guess?"

"It was sort of boring," said Jeremy, "except for the food fight."

"The food fight? You had a food fight? I thought this was supposed to be a fancy party. People had to wear good clothes and all."

"It was," said Fonz. "And they did. But it wasn't."

"To start with," said Jeremy, "the disc jockey was sixteen, a friend of Tobi Jo's older brother, and this was his first job. He kept trying to sound like the guys on the radio."

"But he didn't," said Fonz. "He just sounded stupid. And he didn't have many tapes. He kept playing the same songs over and over."

Jeremy nodded. "And he kept saying, 'Let's mingle, kids. Let's mingle.' But we didn't."

"What do you mean?" I said.

"Well," said Fonz, "the girls were on one side of the room, smiling at us and fixing each other's hair, and we were on the other side of the room telling jokes and talking baseball and daring each other to take our neckties off."

"Except for Rand," said Jeremy. "He mingled."

"With Mary Ellen, I bet," I said.

"And everyone else. He socialized enough for all of us."

Jeremy looked at my nose through squinted eyes. "It doesn't look too swollen."

"It is," I said, "and it hurts. I have to breathe through my mouth. Tell me about the food fight. I can't believe you had a food fight at somebody's party! And dressed in your good clothes!"

"Yeah," said Jeremy. "I got my blazer smeared with onion dip when someone threw a potato chip at me. A potato chip! My mother was not happy."

"I got deviled egg on my shirt," said Fonz. He stared at me. "Did you know that your eye's all yellow and green and blue?"

"Will you guys tell me?" I screamed.

"It happened sort of accidentally," Jeremy said. "First Rand discovered a bowl of peanuts. 'What a

53

shame Jase isn't here,' he said. 'Peanuts for the peanut.' "

"He said that?" I was angry.

"Don't get mad at me," Jeremy said. "I'm only telling the story."

"So tell."

"Mr. and Mrs Joiner brought in trays of all kinds of food just about this time. There were veggies and dip, little sandwiches, chips, candy, cheese and crackers. It looked like a tea party, if you want to know the truth. Anyway, somebody flipped a peanut and somebody else threw it back and things just sort of took off. Before you knew it, guys were throwing cheese hunks and veggies and even those little sandwiches, though the sandwiches didn't throw very well."

"The chips were the worst, though," said Fonz. "I tried, but they were too light."

"So it was you who threw the chip and dip at me," said Jeremy.

The guys looked at each other and grinned. They had had a wonderful time.

"Then Tobi Jo started screaming," said Fonz. "She didn't like us trashing her party, I guess."

"Her father came running," said Jeremy, "and if looks would kill, us guys would all be dead. He was so mad! He comforted Tobi Jo and all the screaming girls and made us guys all go home."

"Poor Tobi Jo," I said and started laughing. "Did guys really throw sandwiches? And deviled eggs?"

54

"And cookies," said Jeremy. "I got hit in the head by a chocolate chip."

"And you didn't feel bad or have a guilty conscience or anything?" I asked.

Fonz thought for a moment. "Not yet. But when my mother hears the whole story, she'll do her best to make me sorry."

"Nobody's mom is going to let them have a party for a long, long time when word of this gets around," I said.

"Good," said Jeremy. "It was stupid. Who wants to go to a party like you were an adult when you're still twelve? I'm not even thirteen until June, for Pete's sake."

"Don't you want to be grown-up?" I asked Jeremy.

"Oh, sure," he said. "I want to drive and have my own money and do what I want to when I want to. I just don't want to go to dumb parties and get dressed up when it's not a wedding or a funeral."

"You don't want to be grown-up ever if it makes you like my parents," Mike said as he charged into my room. His ears were red, so I knew he was upset.

"What are they doing now?" I asked.

"Mom's told Dad he has to leave, and she's helping him by taking all his clothes and throwing them out the front door. He refuses to leave and is picking everything up and stuffing it back in the closet and drawers as fast as she's throwing it out."

Mike looked confused. "How do they expect me to grow up normal if they behave like this?"

"Why did they marry each other?" asked Jeremy.

"Who knows?" said Mike. "I'm sure they've forgotten."

"So," said Fonz, "you can be a kid asked to behave like an adult—like us at Tobi Jo's party—and it doesn't work well. Or you can be an adult and act like a kid—like Mr. and Mrs. Viders—and it doesn't work well either."

"But God is still there," Mike said to no one in particular. "Even when things don't go the way you want, God is there."

Jeremy and Fonz and I looked at each other. We weren't sure if Mike was trying to convince us or himself.

"If that weren't true," Mike said reflectively, "I don't know what I'd do."

8

On Monday there was a little white envelope on my desk, an interesting way to begin a new week. I opened it and pulled out the invitation. PARTY! it said in letters formed of red ribbon. The card was covered with colorful confetti. I opened it to see who it was from.

Judy Post.

Judy Post?

I reread the card. It still said the same thing.

I was so surprised that I looked over at her. She was watching me.

"Thanks," I said insincerely. "I'll have to ask my mom."

She nodded. "You don't have to dress up."

I stashed the invitation in my notebook, hopefully before anyone saw it. I didn't know what to do. I knew I didn't want to go, but I knew I probably should. I needed to think about this.

I told Mr. Andretti I'd be late for track practice because Mr. Keefer wanted me to audition for a solo in the spring concert.

Mr. Keefer had given Heidi and me music so we could practice for the tryouts. I'd gone over it a few times. It wasn't very difficult, just challenging enough to make it interesting.

When I got to Mr. Keefer's room, Heidi hadn't arrived yet.

"Why don't you play, Jase?" Mr. Keefer said. "I know you want to get to track as soon as you can."

He sat down at the piano to accompany me and began running his hands up and down the keys. Beautiful music poured out. I'd been taking piano lessons from Mr. Abbott, a friend of Mr. Keefer's, for several months now. Maybe someday I'd be able to play like Mr. Keefer.

I raised my trumpet to my lips and blew. I loved playing my trumpet. The brass sound was so clear and fine when blown right. I tried to do it right, and only flubbed slightly a couple of times.

"Very nicely done, Jase," said Mr. Keefer. "Very nice indeed." He was smiling broadly.

I put my trumpet back in its case with high hopes for the solo.

Heidi came running in as I clicked my case shut.

She was wearing such bright fire engine red lip-stick that I expected water to squirt out of her mouth when she opened it. She grabbed a tissue and rubbed the red goo off, leaving her mouth all funny and puffy.

I decided to wait while she played. I wanted to hear my competition.

Unfortunately for me, I never heard her play better. She had been practicing! The golden notes still hung in the air as I walked away. I knew before Mr. Keefer said anything that Heidi would be the soloist, not me.

With a funny feeling in the pit of my stomach, I changed for track. No one had ever beaten me in music before.

I was still feeling funny at dinner when Mom surprised me and made me forget all about Heidi.

"I hear you got another party invitation," she said.

"Another?" said Matty. "Wow! You're setting a high social standard for me to follow, you know."

"Don't I just wish," I told her. "How'd you hear about Judy's party, Mom?"

"I met her mother at the grocery store. She said Judy's very excited about Saturday night." Mom looked at my unhappy face. "I take it you aren't."

"Mom," I said, deciding to be honest, "I don't want to go to Judy's party."

Mom looked at me with one eyebrow cocked, a bad sign. "Why not? You wanted to go to Tobi Jo's."

"Judy's . . ." I stopped and searched for a word that

would be gentle enough not to make my mother mad. "Judy's . . ."

"Unpopular?" suggested Mom. "Shy and awkward? Not pretty?"

"Yes!" I said, delighted she understood. "Yes, yes!"

"All the more reason for you to go," she said firmly.

I looked at her sadly because I knew she was right.

"Put yourself in Judy's place," said Mom. "What if you gave a party and no one came?"

"It's only one evening, Jase," said Dad.

Matty looked at me and smiled sympathetically.

"Not only will you be doing the right thing," said Mom, "but you'll be making Judy happy."

Since when was it my job to make Judy happy? But I knew they were right and I'd go. Judy had enough problems without me making them worse by being selfish.

On Thursday we had a track meet with Concord. It was a sunny day, and I was looking forward to the events.

I'd already won a victory that day. Mr. Keefer had sent for me in the morning. I'd gone to see him in the music room knowing he was going to tell me Heidi had won the solo. In fact, I beat him to it.

"Heidi got the solo, didn't she?"

He nodded. "You've got to agree that she did extremely well."

I nodded glumly.

"However," Mr. Keefer continued, "you did very

well, too. So I've decided to give you both solos. Heidi will play the one you both auditioned for and you will play another. There's not time for the whole band to learn another piece, so would you mind playing with only me accompanying?"

I was so surprised I could hardly answer. "T-that would be great, Mr. Keefer," I stammered.

I floated about a foot in the air all day, and now I was more than ready for my first track event, the 100-yard dash. The starter's pistol fired and I raced down the track. I could barely remember the time I felt like I was running in slow motion. Today I ate up the ground in great bites and hit the tape first. What a fabulous feeling! Even Rand's crack about Mighty Mouse McCarver couldn't dim my joy.

Earlier this week we'd beaten Upper Gulph, and today we were hoping for our fifth straight win.

My 400-meter relay team was not very good, but we tried. We ran hard and only fumbled one baton pass, and we came in fourth out of six teams.

My 800-meter relay team had become very special, a wonderful team. I ran the first leg and passed the baton to Jeremy who passed to a guy named Gary who passed to a guy named Warren. When no one flubbed the baton pass, we were almost impossible to beat.

I took my sweats off and took my place for this race. I clutched the baton in my right hand as I set myself on the blocks, seat high, eyes ahead.

Waiting for me 200 meters ahead was Jeremy.

The starter's pistol fired and I was off. I ran as hard as I could at Jeremy who was jogging in place, watching me, and still wearing his sweats.

I blinked. *He was still wearing his sweats! Nobody raced in sweats!*

Jeremy realized he had his sweats on at about the same time I did. I went into the curve of the track just as Jeremy pulled his jacket off. He tossed it on the grass just as I pulled enough ahead of the other runners in my leg to lose them in my side vision.

Jeremy pulled one leg out of his pants, but there was no way he'd get the other out before I reached him.

"Jeremy!" I screamed.

He looked up and saw me almost on top of him. I held out the baton in my right hand.

Jeremy grabbed his empty sweat pant leg in one hand and the baton in the other and ran. He looked absolutely ridiculous. He would definitely join Mike and me in the Keystone Junior High Track Team Hall of Fame.

Somehow, in spite of Jeremy, our relay team still won, and so did Keystone.

"It was a great meet, Mr. McCarver," Mike said as he ate dinner with us. "But the best part was Jeremy. There he was, one leg on, one leg off, zipping right along just like he knew what he was doing."

Mike took a dinner roll and popped it in his mouth. He always inhaled these huge meals when he ate with us. I think it was because his mother rarely had time to cook, and homemade dinners tasted great to him.

"When's your election, Jase?" asked Matty. He was staring at his meat loaf, trying to get up nerve to eat a piece.

"Next week. My speech is tomorrow and the election's next week."

"What are your chances of winning?" The kid took a deep breath and forced himself to put some meat loaf in his mouth. By his face, it looked like he was eating poison instead of one of my favorites.

"It's hard to say what's going to happen," I said. "Most kids either don't say who they're for or they keep changing their minds."

"Does Rand have any posters or badges or anything yet?" Matty took a big gulp of milk to wash down the meat loaf.

"Only his ERASE JASE masterpiece."

Matty drowned his second piece of meat loaf in catsup. "Maybe we can make him some."

Dad and Mom both lit up.

"Just one minute," I said, unpleasantly jolted by my brother's suggestion. "Why are you helping my competition? Don't you want me to win?"

"Oh, Jase, of course," said Mom, patting my hand. "You're certainly more important to us than Rand. We won't do this project if you think we shouldn't. Mike, have some more macaroni and cheese?"

Mike took a big spoonful and another slice of meat loaf, too.

"Mrs. McCarver," he said around a mouthful,

"Rand really is mean sometimes, especially to Jase. I can understand why he doesn't want you to help him."

Mom nodded. "We know. And we think Jase has done a fine job of putting up with Rand's tricks."

"It's interesting to me," said Mike, looking disappointed because the rolls were gone, "how you guys try to be nice to Rand and want Jase to be nice to him even though most of the time he's not nice back. My mom and dad act like mean should be followed by meaner and still meaner."

"Nice is nicer," said Matty. "That's what Christians try to do." He pushed his last two bites of meat loaf around on his plate. "Mom?" he said hopefully.

"Only two more, Matty," she said. "You can do it."

He sighed and in an abrupt change of topic asked Mike, "Are you going to Judy Post's party Saturday night?"

I could have strangled Matty! I waited for Mike's ears to turn red. Instead I got a real surprise.

Mike said, "I don't know. I'm not much of a party animal."

"You got invited?" I said, trying not to let my surprise show too much.

Mike nodded. "Are you going?"

I glanced at Mom. "Yes."

"I'll go with you," Mike offered. "Who else is going?"

"I don't know. I haven't heard anybody talk about it!"

64

"Mrs. Post told me Judy asked about twenty-five people, but she didn't mention any names," said Mom.

Mike looked impressed. "That's quite a party."

"Apparently she felt badly about not being asked to Tobi Jo's, so she's having her own." Mom handed Mike a bowl of ice cream for dessert. "Have some, Mike?"

Silly question.

9

I had spent the whole week worrying about my speech to the seventh grade. I hated talking in front of a group. I didn't mind running a race or playing my trumpet in front of any number of people, but even thinking about speaking made me break out in a sweat.

The morning of the fateful Friday, Mom looked me over very carefully before I left for school. She was more interested in how I was dressed than I was.

"Image is very important in politics, Jase," she said.

"Mom, this is the seventh grade, not politics." I looked down at the gray slacks and navy blazer she was making me wear.

"Let me straighten your tie," she said, fiddling

around at my neck, practically choking me. "The tail is so long, dear," she said. "Shouldn't you retie it?"

"I can retie it forever, and it won't make any difference. It's Dad's tie and it will always be too long." I pulled away from her and adjusted the tie so I could breathe. I grabbed the doorknob. "The bus, Mom. I'll miss the bus."

When I flopped into my seat beside Mike, I was a wreck. I did not want to give this speech! At that moment I didn't even want to be mayor. My nerves were jumping up and down all over my body, making me feel like a big lump of quivery Jell-O.

I saw Mike looking me over, getting ready to make a comment on my clothes. I scowled at him.

"Don't say a word if you value your life," I snarled.

He went back to his computer magazine with a huge smile. At least someone was enjoying today.

They made Mary Ellen, Rand, and me sit on the stage and face everybody. It was weird. Some kids smiled at us, some made faces, some laughed and pointed. Jeremy, Fonz, and Mike gave me a thumbs-up sign which helped me feel a little better . . . not much, just a little better.

Mary Ellen got to give her speech first for two reasons. She was a girl ("Ladies first") and Lafferty came before McCarver and Purcell alphabetically.

"Radley Park is very special to me," she said. "We moved here from Philadelphia when I was in third grade. I enjoy the country living out here. I like my friends out here. I like my school out here. To be

Radley Park's Mayor for a Day would be a great honor."

Everybody clapped enthusiastically, especially the girls.

I stood up, telling my knees not to let me down. I walked to the podium without tripping. It was such a relief that I smiled, and the audience actually smiled back.

"You could vote for the prettiest," I said, and everybody looked at Mary Ellen. "You could vote for the biggest." And everyone looked at Rand. "Or you could vote for the best." I paused and smiled here just like Dad had told me. "And I would certainly appreciate your support."

I sat down to laughter and applause and a stomach that no longer felt tied in knots.

Rand strode to the podium like it was his own personal piece of furniture.

"We all know how important it is to vote. Politicians tell us so all the time. So be certain you vote . . . for *me* as Radley Park's Mayor for a Day. That way you get the handsomest, biggest, and best all in one."

He looked at me and smiled triumphantly while the kids all clapped loudly.

I shivered. What if he actually beat me?

That night we went miniature golfing with the church youth group. Rand came along, too, thanks to my father.

Mike and I had jumped in the car after track practice and said, "Hurry up, Dad. We'll be late if we don't get a move on it. We have to be there in less than an hour and we have to shower and eat first."

"Where are you going?" Rand asked as he climbed into the front seat.

"Miniature golfing," I said. "With church."

"Have you ever played miniature golf?" Dad asked Rand.

He shook his head.

"Come along then," said Dad.

Rand looked back at me. "Is Mary Ellen going?"

I felt like lying, but I knew I couldn't. "Yes."

"Ask your mother when we get to your house," said Dad.

"My mom won't be home until very late tonight. I can go if I want." He was quiet until we pulled up to his empty house. He looked at it, then turned to Dad. "What time would you pick me up?"

Now he was playing with Pastor Tony and two other guys. His golf club looked awfully small in his huge hand.

Mary Ellen had brought Tobi Jo with her. They played with Sally and Pastor Tony's wife, Laura. I made certain my group of Mike, Jeremy, and Fonz, was right behind the girls so I could be near Mary Ellen and maybe even speak to her. While we were waiting for our turn to start, I found myself beside Mary Ellen and Tobi Jo. I couldn't believe my luck.

"How's your eye doing?" Mary Ellen asked. "Does it still hurt?"

I shook my head, delighted she cared enough to ask. "It's fine."

"But did you notice how well his navy blazer matched his black eye when he gave his speech to-day?" asked Mike. "He was color coordinated."

"Tobi Jo," I said, ignoring Mike, "I meant to tell you I was sorry I had to miss your party last week. I heard it was great."

To my horror, Tobi Jo's face turned red and her eyes filled with tears as she turned and walked away.

"Jase!" Mary Ellen said. "How could you!" She stamped her foot and a tiny pouf of dust exploded. I think she'd have kicked me in the shins if she'd dared. She spun around and marched off after Tobi Jo, her chin held high.

"What'd I do?" I asked the guys. "I was trying to be nice."

Mike, Jeremy, and Fonz were laughing at me.

"Boy, are you dumb!" said Jeremy. "The worst night in the girl's life, and you casually bring it up like it was nothing."

"Oh." Of course. I felt like jerk of the year.

"I guess you had to be there," said Fonz, "to understand the night from Tobi Jo's point of view. It was a clear case of things not going the way you want."

"So's this," I said. "Now I'll have to apologize for my apology."

"A piece of advice," said Jeremy. "Don't mention it again ever in your whole life. Come on; it's our turn to play."

I liked miniature golf. My family played it often when we went to the New Jersey shore for our vacations. Mike, in contrast, had never played.

"How do you hold this thing?" he asked, waving his club around.

"Like this," said Jeremy, whose dad played lots and lots of golf.

Mike tried to copy Jeremy's hand position. "Now what?"

"Swing gently but firmly."

"Like this?" Mike swatted at his ball and topped it. It rolled maybe a foot. It took him eight shots to get the ball in the cup, and then he was successful only because Jeremy stood with his feet spread behind the hole to guide the ball in.

At the next hole, Mike got a six. "I'm getting it," he said proudly. "I'm getting it."

The third hole, he hit his ball just right. It disappeared up the drawbridge of a little castle and got spit out a side window with just enough stuff to roll into the cup for a hole in one. I thought Jeremy, Fonz, and I would die laughing.

By the second nine holes, Tobi Jo seemed to be feeling better. Her curls were going SPROING again. I decided Jeremy was right; I wouldn't risk apologizing a second time.

At the twelfth hole I smiled at Mary Ellen as we waited our turn. She half-smiled back and then went and stood by Tobi Jo. I decided I'd better keep my shins protected for a little while longer.

The fifteenth hole was a tower of boxes with a little plank going uphill into the second box. There were also skinny ground level paths on either side of the box tower. You were supposed to go up the plank into the second box and pop out on another plank on the side. Then the ball would roll down that plank into the cup.

I watched the guys all try to get up the plank. No one could do it, not even Jeremy who was beating us all. I decided I'd go up the side path instead. If I banked my shot off the side rail just right, the ball would come out very near the hole. I'd just need a lot of power on the shot.

I swung hard and the ball flew down the little path beside the box tower. It struck the side rail exactly where I'd aimed, but instead of rolling obediently toward the hole, it took off like a low line drive. I never even got to yell, "Look out!"

It hit Mary Ellen right on her ankle bone. One minute she was laughing at something Sally had said. The next she was on the ground, holding her ankle and trying not to cry.

"Mary Ellen!" I dropped my golf club and ran to her.

Laura, Pastor Tony's wife, was there first. She sat on the ground beside Mary Ellen and checked to see if she was badly hurt. I could only stand and stare and feel awful. Did ankle bones break easily?

"Can you stand?" Laura finally asked the tearful Mary Ellen. She and Sally helped Mary Ellen to her feet, and she tried to take a step. She limped but she didn't fall.

"It hurts, but it holds me," she said. She wiped at her eyes and sniffed. "But I don't think I want to finish the game."

"There's a bench by the entrance," said Laura. "You can sit there. Sally and Jase, help Mary Ellen while I get one of those chemical ice packs from the first-aid kit in the church van."

"I'll take care of her." Rand suddenly appeared and put his hand under Mary Ellen's elbow.

"Thank you, Rand," said both Laura and Mary Ellen.

As if I didn't feel badly enough, I had to stand and watch Rand-the-hero help Mary Ellen to the bench by the entrance and sit there with her until we were ready to leave. My score on the last three holes was so terrible even Mike beat me.

While everybody was turning in their golf clubs and comparing scores, I sat beside Mary Ellen on her bench. I did my best to ignore Rand on her other side.

"How's your ankle?" I asked.

She held it out, and we both looked at it. It was swollen and already a massive bruise was forming.

"I'm sorry," I said, twisting my golf club in my hands. "I didn't mean to hurt you."

Mary Ellen smiled faintly.

"Hey, Jase, give me your club," called Mike. "I'll turn it in for you."

I offered my club to Mike just as Mary Ellen

lowered her foot, and the two met with a "clonk" as the metal head bounced off her injured ankle.

"I'm sorry! I'm sorry!" I yelled.

Mary Ellen's face was all scrunched up in pain and anger as she grabbed her ankle again.

"I'm sorry," I repeated. I knew I'd never forgive myself. "I didn't mean it."

"I'm sure you didn't," she said through clenched teeth.

I started to relax.

"But you still did it. You're not very smart sometimes, Jase."

My smile shriveled.

"You say things and do things that hurt. I don't know whether you plan it or not, but you do it."

My mouth fell open at the unfair attack. Plan it? To hurt her of all people?

"Either way, just keep away from me . . . and Tobi Jo!"

It wouldn't have been quite so painful to be chopped in little pieces if I hadn't seen Rand grinning at me the whole time.

"Come on," he said kindly, taking Mary Ellen's arm. "Let's erase Jase."

Very carefully Rand helped Mary Ellen into the church van. Feeling like melted ice cubes, I climbed into the other van with the guys.

On the way home, we stopped at the Guernsey Cow, a dairy bar that had great sundaes and ice-cream sodas. I felt so terrible I didn't even care if I had anything.

"This is serious, Jase. When you don't eat ice cream, we're in trouble. Order," Mike said.

I sat.

"Order!" he ordered.

I sat.

"A banana split for this guy . . . and one for me," Mike told the waitress.

While I waited for the ice cream I felt I could never get down my throat, I went to the men's room to rinse my face in cold water. Maybe then it would stop burning with embarrassment.

I walked past Mary Ellen who had her foot up on a chair. She made believe she didn't see me.

I was drying my hands when I saw Jeremy's foot sticking out from under one of the stalls. I tiptoed over to the foot and stomped on it as hard as I could. Stunned silence was Jeremy's only response.

I couldn't shake Mary Ellen or attack Rand, so I stomped on my friend Jeremy instead. It wasn't a very nice thing to do, but I felt better after I did it. I ran out of the room as quickly as I could so he wouldn't know who had done it.

When I got back to the table, I was grinning broadly.

"Well, look who's lost the glums," said Mike. "What are you laughing about?"

"I just stomped on Jeremy's foot and he doesn't know it was me."

75

Mike stared at me, then looked to his right. There sat Jeremy, stuffing his face with the free pretzels on each table.

"Oops!" I said, slapping my hand over my mouth. "You're here!"

"I've been here ever since we got here," Jeremy said.

"Then who'd I step on? Who's got sneakers like you?"

We all looked at the men's room just as the door opened and a frowning Rand walked out.

"Oh, no!" I almost choked on a pretzel.

We all leaned in our seats to try and see Rand's sneakers. Then we swiveled to look at Jeremy's. They matched.

"But didn't you notice the foot was bigger than usual?" Jeremy gasped between laughs.

"Now that you mention it, it was quite large."

When our sundaes came, we could hardly eat them, we were giggling so. When I glanced at Mary Ellen, she was glaring at us. I gave a little wave. She sniffed and turned away. I felt terrible that she was still mad at me, but I couldn't stop laughing.

None of us dared look at Rand.

"Don't tell anyone what I did," I pleaded between laughs. "He'd kill me."

"This is blackmailable action," said Mike. "We've got you in our power forever?"

We were still snickering when we got back into the

van the church had rented for the evening. We didn't stop until Pastor Tony pulled the van to the side of the back country road he was taking for a shortcut and said, "I think we've got a flat."

10

We piled out of the van and stared at the flat. The night was dark with no moon, and the tire was nearly invisible, but we all looked at it anyway. There were seven of us kids and Pastor Tony.

When Pastor Tony finally found the jack and put it in place, he was most unhappy.

"This thing doesn't work! Every time it goes up a notch, it comes back down two!"

"Let me try," said Fonz. "I help my Uncle Charlie at his garage a lot."

"No, Fonz." Pastor Tony shook his head. "I appreciate your offer, but this is too unsafe. I can't let any of you kids help. What we need to do is call Laura and have her bring the church van. Then we can use that jack."

I turned in a circle, scanning the area. Pastor Tony must have picked his short-cut for loneliness. There wasn't a house in sight, just woods and fields.

"There's a house just down the road," said Jeremy, pointing back the way we'd come.

"You're sure?" Pastor Tony asked.

"Yep. Their mailbox was a little wooden barn with BARNES written on it. I remember because that's my name, too."

"How did you see this in the dark?" Fonz asked.

"The headlights, you goof. The writing was white on this little red barn."

"Okay, troops," said Pastor Tony. "Let's go visit the Barnes's family." He locked the van and started up the road.

Sure enough, Jeremy was right. We came to the barn mailbox in no time. The house itself sat way back on a big, big lawn. Pastor Tony marched up the drive with us behind him, giggling and whispering and shoving each other.

"Quiet, guys," Pastor Tony said.

We giggled harder.

Suddenly the lamppost to my right burst into light, and I jumped a mile. We all giggled some more.

Pastor Tony turned to us and hushed us. "I'm going to ask this man if I can use his phone. You guys stay here quietly. There's no use making him think he's being invaded."

Pastor Tony rang the doorbell, and a porch light came on to bathe him in brightness.

79

I couldn't see the door open, but I could hear Pastor Tony say, "Hello. I'm Tony Himmel. I was driving a rented van when I had a flat right down the road here." He pointed toward the van. "The jack provided with the van doesn't work well at all. May I use your phone to call my wife? She could bring our van which has a good jack in it."

Pastor Tony stood as though he were listening to an answer though we couldn't hear any words.

"I'm a youth pastor," Pastor Tony said. "These are some of my junior high kids. We've been miniature golfing."

There was another brief pause. Whatever the man said, I could tell by Pastor Tony's face that it was unexpected.

"Well," he said, "then would you mind calling my wife for me? I'll give you the number."

"He won't let Pastor Tony use his phone," hissed Mike. "He must be scared of us."

"All you have to do is call her." Pastor Tony's voice was raised. "Please!"

It wasn't a loud slam, but it was a firm slam. Immediately the porch light and the driveway lamp went out.

"Now what?" Mike asked as Pastor Tony joined us. We weren't giggling at all now. "Talk about things not going the way you'd want them to go!"

"But the Lord is still with us and cares about how we react," Pastor Tony said as if to remind himself. He still looked a little stunned by Mr. Barnes's unpleasant behavior. "I guess we'll just have to work with the jack we have."

It took more than thirty nervous minutes to get the tire changed. The jack was very unstable, but Pastor Tony finally managed to get the van raised enough to lift the wheel off the road. Things moved quickly then.

When we pulled into the church parking lot, there were several cars of concerned parents waiting and one very concerned youth pastor's wife. Everyone was very understanding when Pastor Tony explained what had happened.

The guys and I climbed into our car to find Dad and Rand deep in conversation. I frowned. Not only was my worst enemy impressing my would-be girlfriend while I was doing just the opposite, but he and my father were becoming friends. All the embarrassments of the evening were flashing in neon in my mind.

When we got to Rand's, his house was still dark and empty.

"Would you like me to come in with you?" Dad asked.

I'd have liked him to come in with me if that were my house. It was all dark and spooky.

"No, thanks. You don't have to," Rand said. "I'm used to being alone here."

"Well, we'll wait until you're in just to make certain everything's okay." Dad slipped the car in park.

"Thanks." Rand's voice had a relieved sound to it.

He waved to Dad but never turned to say good-bye to us guys in the backseat.

"He never said good-bye to us!" I was miffed. Here we gave him a ride, and he never said good-bye.

"He's a hurting kid, Jase," said Dad. "You've got to make allowances."

I watched him as he fumbled with the front door. I felt I spent my whole life making allowances for him.

As lights sprang on all over the house, Dad continued softly, "And don't forget, you never said good-bye to him either."

So now the trouble was my fault.

I went right to bed as soon as I got home, but I couldn't sleep. I kept remembering Tobi Jo's tears and Mary Ellen's ankle, my golf club, and Rand's smirk. I couldn't remember any reason to have laughed all evening.

I got Petey, my parakeet, out of his cage and let him run up and down my stomach as I stared at the ceiling.

God, I thought, *how come I'm always so dumb?*

I didn't hear any answer.

Finally I decided to go get the *Sports Illustrated* I had been reading in the living room. There was a great article in it on this year's pennant possibilities.

When I got out of bed, Petey climbed up my chest to my shoulder, scooted along to my neck and began to tweak my ear. It tickled, and I felt a little less depressed.

Mom and Dad were still up talking when I came

into the living room.

"He is hard to like because he's so cocky," said Dad. "He's his own worst enemy."

"Rand," I said.

Dad nodded. "He and I had a nice talk while we waited for you. He seemed very concerned about Mary Ellen."

I bet he was.

"What did he do?" I asked. "Tell you what a fool you have for a son?" I grabbed the *Sports Illustrated* from the magazine rack.

"Jase!" said Mom. "That's no way to talk about yourself!"

"We never mentioned you, Jase," said Dad. "We talked about the difficulties in his life. He has some hard problems to deal with right now."

"What?" I said. "Rand has difficulties? Aside from his mother, everything goes right for him! He's tall, he's handsome, the girls love him, he gets good grades, he's probably going to beat me for Mayor for a Day, and he's one of the best guys on the track team. Nothing goes right for him? Hah! I could tell you about things not going right! I could tell you about making a fool of yourself! But I don't want to talk about it, so I won't. Good night!"

Startled, Mom and Dad watched me storm out of the room. Now they could talk about me instead of Rand.

When I flopped on my bed, Petey, who had been sitting on my pajama collar, squawked loudly because

83

I almost squished him. He climbed to my forehead and began chewing me out.

"Quiet, Bird," I said. "I have enough problems without you getting mad at me too."

Petey climbed onto the headboard and stared down at me like a miniature vulture waiting for a good meal. He looked like a feathery version of Snoopy. I had to smile.

Suddenly a thought hit me.

I had troubles.

Rand had troubles.

Mike had troubles.

Tobi Jo had troubles.

Mary Ellen had troubles.

Judy Post had troubles.

Did everyone have troubles of some kind? Was it possible that things didn't go right for everybody? Did we all ask God why we were so dumb?

What an unbelievable situation if we all felt the same way!

11

On Saturday night Mom dropped us at Judy's with the promise that she would come for us by ten. Kindness this night was a curfew.

When Judy answered the door, she had on a pink something-or-other, and she almost looked pretty. Her hair was curled, and she had on some pink cheek stuff and some lipstick.

"Come in," she said, and backed up to make room for us. When she stepped back, she stepped on her cat who hissed and ran away. Judy jumped and blushed and looked more like usual.

"This is my mom," she said.

I stared at the very pretty lady who was standing in the living room. This was Judy's mom?

The doorbell rang and Judy went to answer it. Her mother watched her with a smile.

"She reminds me of myself at that age," said Mrs. Post.

"Really?" I said, unable to believe Mrs. Post had ever been thirteen, let alone a frowsy thirteen like Judy.

Mrs. Post looked at me like she knew exactly what I was thinking.

"Really," she said. "People change, you know."

Mary Ellen, Sally, and Tobi Jo came into the room with Judy and rescued me from Mrs. Post. I went looking for Mike and found him in the family room gazing lovingly at a personal computer. I could see his hands twitch with the desire to play with it.

"Want to play a game or two?" asked a tall older kid who came rushing in the back door. "Let me get a couple of good ones for you."

He pulled a large plastic storage unit of floppy discs off a shelf.

"Our games," he said.

Mike's eyes bulged. He'd never seen so many at once outside a store. Neither had I.

"Greg," said Judy as she and the girls came into the room, "you promised me you'd keep the computer off!"

Greg pointed at Mike. "He was drooling over the thing. I was just trying to be nice."

"Keep on being nice," said Mike. "Please!"

"This person is my brother Greg," said Judy. "He's

86

a junior in high school, and he plays trumpet in the band, Jase."

All of us but Mike played for Mr. Keefer, and we knew the high school band was BIG-TIME STUFF.

"Did you march in the cavalcade competition last year when Radley Park won the state championship?" I asked.

Greg nodded. "It was the greatest thing ever! We also got to march in the Orange Bowl Parade and at Disney World this year."

BIG-TIME STUFF.

Next thing I knew we were watching Mr. Post's videos of the state competition, the Orange Bowl Parade and Disney World. Greg fast-forwarded past all the extra things and just showed us the Radley Park Royal Raiders Marching Band in their royal purple and cream uniforms piped in gold. They were great!

"Look at those straight lines," said Greg proudly. "And look at our trumpets. Every trumpet is held at the exact same angle!"

"I wonder where they'll go when it's our turn?" I asked.

"I don't care," said Sally. "I'll go anywhere they'll take me. I just want to be in the band front. I want to whip those rifles around."

"Not me," said Tobi Jo. "I want to be a majorette." She started twisting her wrist, twirling an imaginary baton. "I've been taking lessons for years."

"She's won a bunch of medals," said Mary Ellen.

87

We were all properly impressed.

"I'll just march with the flutes," said Mary Ellen.

"And me with the trumpets," I said. "Too bad you'll be gone when I get there," I told Greg.

"What about you, Judy?" asked Sally.

Judy blushed and looked very self-conscious. "I'd like to be in the flag line," she said.

"She'd like to be captain of the flags," said Greg. "She goes to all the cavalcades and watches the flag captain like a hawk."

Judy got redder and looked unhappy that Greg had revealed her dream.

"Do bands have managers like sports teams?" asked Mike. "I can manage, at least until I'm ready to be drum major." He pointed to the very tall, very skinny Raider in the high beaver hat strutting in front of the band. We all laughed at the thought of Dough Boy Mike as a drum major.

After the Royal Raiders were finished marching, we watched some old cartoons and comedy shorts that were a riot. I played Mike in a game of Flight Fight and got creamed while the girls practiced some cheers. Judy was pretty good.

"Tryouts for cheerleaders for next year are Monday," said Mary Ellen.

"I know," said Judy. "I might go."

"Hah!" said Greg. "You've been practicing for months!"

Judy flushed again. For the first time I appreciated what a trial big brothers could be. Poor Matty.

Tobi Jo challenged Mike to a game of computer chess and almost beat him while we watched a Mighty Mouse cartoon in reverse. I was glad Rand wasn't there to make any Mighty Mouse jokes. Mike did his famous Rand impersonation, and Mary Ellen laughed so hard she cried. I had a wonderful time when Greg let me play with his synthesizer. It made the greatest noises!

At 9:30 the doorbell rang, and a guy delivered several pizzas. That was when two things hit me. I was having fun at Judy Post's house, and none of the twenty-five invited people had come to the party except Mary Ellen, Sally, Tobi Jo, Mike, and me.

12

On Monday Dad took me to school early. I carried a paper bag that held a stack of posters for Rand. Mom and Dad and Matty had spent yesterday afternoon making ISN'T HE GRAND? LET'S VOTE FOR RAND posters.

I'd even gotten carried away and made one that read STRIKE UP THE BAND AND GO VOTE FOR RAND. I'd cut out pictures of imstruments and pasted them all over the poster. However, if I had anything to say about anything, Rand would never find out I made it. In fact, he'd never find out who made any of them.

I took the posters to Rand's homeroom and got out of there before anyone saw me.

I was watching for Rand's bus when I saw Judy. She looked like her usual preparty self, afraid and uncertain, wrinkled even though her clothes were permanent press. I had sort of expected that she'd look better because she had looked so nice for her Saturday night party. Obviously, I was wrong.

"Hi, Judy," I said. "I had fun Saturday night."

She looked at me without lifting her head, sort of pushing her eyeballs way high.

"No, you didn't," she said.

I blinked. "Yes, I did."

"No, you didn't. You're just saying that to be nice."

"No, I'm not." Her attitude made me angry. "What's the matter? Do you think I'm lying or something?"

"I'd believe that before I'd believe you had a good time."

While I was staring at her, Mike walked up.

"Hey, Judy," he said. "Saturday night was great."

"No, it wasn't," she said.

Now it was Mike's turn to blink.

"All you liked was my brother's computer," Judy said. She turned and walked to her homeroom, her head down and her arms wrapped around her books like they were precious.

"I've heard that girls get moody," said Mike, "but this is ridiculous."

Just then I saw Rand get off his bus and go to his locker. I trailed him to his homeroom, then stood in the doorway like I was looking for someone. I watched him discover the bag, look at it strangely, then pull out the posters. He stared at the top one, then began flipping through them. He turned to the guy in the next seat and said something. The guy just shook his head no. So did all the kids around him.

He looked completely confused as he took them to the teacher, Mrs. Stevens. She nodded, pulled out some thumbtacks and gave them to him. He left the room frowning, almost running into me and not even on purpose. I don't think he saw me.

When I returned to my room a few minutes later, I saw ISN'T HE GRAND? hanging beside JASE SET THE PACE and WE'RE ALL YELLIN'—VOTE FOR MARY ELLEN.

At lunch, I went to Mary Ellen's table. I usually wouldn't have the nerve to do something like this, especially since I still wasn't her favorite person, but Judy had me puzzled.

"Mary Ellen, what's the matter with Judy?" I asked.

She looked at Sally and Tobi Jo.

"Has she been nasty to you, too?" asked Sally.

"She told me I was a liar when I said I had a nice time Saturday night. Mike says she's just moody."

The girls all nodded.

"That's it?" I said.

"That's it," say Mary Ellen. "We think she got to thinking about all the kids who didn't come and it made her feel really bad."

"But that's not our fault," I said. "We're the ones

that Judy should be nice to."

"Hi, Beautiful. Hi, Little Jase." Rand slid onto the bench beside Mary Ellen and forced her to make room for him. I hadn't had the nerve to do that. "I hear you folks went to Judy Post's bash Saturday night. What was it—Be Kind to Our Webfooted Friends Night or something?"

"Rand!" said Mary Ellen. "That was nasty! How could you?"

For once it was my turn to grin while Rand got chewed out. It was wonderful.

"Okay, okay," he said, holding up a hand. "I'm sorry. Now I have to ask you a question. Did you do it?"

Mary Ellen looked confused. "What?"

"Make those posters for me?"

"Are you kidding? You're my competition!"

"I did it. I confess," I said.

"Sure, Mighty Mouse. Sure." Rand sneered at me.

I vowed I'd go home and practice curling my lip so I could scoff back. As I walked back to my seat, I tried a sneer.

"What's the matter? Smell something bad?" asked Mike.

I was going to need a lot of practice.

It was raining at the end of the school day, so we had track practice in the gym. While we were stretching and bending, Mrs. Kyroni, the girls' phys. ed. teacher and cheerleading coach, walked in with about two dozen girls trailing her. She wasn't happy to see us, but we didn't mind the girls.

The track team was divided into three groups. One group was to run the halls, another to practice sprints the length of the gym, and the third was to practice baton passing on the other side of the gym.

Mrs. Kyroni and the girls ended up in one corner where those who were already cheerleaders taught the cheers to those who wanted to be cheerleaders.

"Just make believe the track team isn't here!" I heard Mrs. Kyroni yell once. Easier said than done.

I was sent out to run the halls.

"Don't come back until you're sweating like a pig," Mr. Zindorf told us.

"What's a pig sweat like?" asked Jeremy as we set off.

"Who knows?" I was jogging along, minding my own business, when suddenly someone stepped on my heel. My sneaker came off and I lurched into a locker.

I knew who was responsible even before I heard him snicker.

I looked up to see Rand going down the hall backwards, waving at me as he laughed.

The temptation to grab all the ISN'T HE GRAND posters and tear them into little, teeny pieces was so strong that I had to clench my fists and grit my teeth. Being nice was a costly thing.

When I returned to the gym some time later, sweating enough to satisfy Mr. Zindorf even if not like a pig, Mary Ellen, Tobi Jo, and Judy were hopping up and down and yelling at the top of their voices.

Mary Ellen looked great; Tobi Jo looked bouncy; and Judy looked like Judy when she'd stepped on her cat. I knew she could do better because I'd seen her the other night, but somehow having an audience made her awkward and jerky.

The girls left before we did, planning to return tomorrow after school for their official, this-one-counts tryouts. If everything went as scheduled, our track team would be in Upland for the last meet of the season and miss the fun. I had good feelings about Mary Ellen and Tobi Jo, but I was very worried about Judy.

13

Upland had a pretty poor track team, and it was a good thing for us. Half of our guys seemed to be out sick.

Derek wasn't there and I got to be the third person in the long jump. Earl and Jeremy jumped nice distances, and then it was my turn. I ran at the line and disqualified myself on my first attempt. The second time I was all right. I didn't have the feeling of sailing like I did the day I bloodied my nose and blackened my eye, but I felt I didn't shame myself either. I was fifth out of six.

I ran the 100-yard dash and won easily. My 400-meter relay team and the other 400 team—the one Fonz was on—combined to field one team. I didn't run with them, and they came in second of two. My 800-meter relay team won, Rand set a meet record with the shot, and Keystone was victorious.

"Don't think you can skip practice for the rest of the week just because our dual season is over," Mr. Andretti told us before he let us off the bus back at school. "The Brandywine Invitational will give you competition like you've never had before. You've got to keep sharp. I expect to see all of you on Wednesday, Thursday, and Friday. No excuses!"

The next morning I asked Mary Ellen, "How did she do?"

She knew who I meant. "Not very well."

"But we know she can do it," I said. "We saw her at her house."

"People seem to make her all elbows and knees. She gets so self-conscious!"

"When will you find out who made it?"

"The list will be posted by the gym at the end of the day."

I nodded. "I hope you're on it."

"I hope so, too." Her red-gold hair shone in the sunlight and her dimple in her right cheek flashed as she smiled. "But if I'm not, I'll live."

"Will Judy?"

Mary Ellen looked thoughtful. "It'll be hard on her."

At lunch Mike, Fonz, and Jeremy helped me with a campaign gimmick my brother thought up.

"Are you the littlest candidate, Jase?" Matty asked.

I snarled in his direction. "You don't have to rub it in!"

"No," he said. "I'm not trying to be mean. I have an idea. Why not take advantage of your size? Get a bunch of peanuts, put a 'J' on them with a felt marker and hand them out at lunch one day."

I thought about the idea, and the more I thought, the more I liked it. I liked the humor of it. I liked the way it showed Rand his cracks about my size didn't bother me. I liked the way it reminded the voters of me.

By the time the guys and I had made the rounds of the lunchroom with the peanuts, everybody was laughing. I couldn't have been more pleased with the response. Mary Ellen laughed with everybody else, but Rand was obviously not happy with my gimmick. He scowled, making a thundercloud look like a rainbow by comparison.

I was walking to my class when Derek passed me going in the opposite direction.

"Got any leftovers for a nonvoter?" he called.

"Welcome back," I said, tossing him a peanut over my shoulder.

Because I wasn't looking where I was going, I didn't even see Rand until I bumped into him. I bounced off, helped along by a hefty shove from his arm. My books and the leftover peanuts went flying everywhere.

So did I, right into Judy Post. Judy's books went every which way, and she went down on her hands

98

and knees. I managed not to fall by hanging onto the drinking fountain.

"Peanuts!" shouted somebody, and the free-for-all was on.

In the process, my books and Judy's got kicked all over and Judy's hand got stepped on.

I know I was embarrassed and my face was scarlet, but Judy looked terrible. She held her injured hand to her chest and her eyes swam with tears. Her hair was all over the place, and her skirt had come up when she fell. One of her shoes had fallen off and been kicked down the hall. Her pocketbook had come open and dumped all over the floor. Now we all knew she had a hairy brush that needed cleaning, a cracked mirror, a pink wallet with a clear change purse on the outside that had three pennies in it, a bunch of dirty tissues, a tiny bottle of perfume, a mystery paperback with a wild cover, and a little bottle of yellow pills, a few of which had tumbled out and gotten stepped on.

When the peanuts were all grabbed up, everybody just stood and stared down at Judy. There was concern on a number of faces, but I knew she felt like a dying rabbit surrounded by wolves.

"Yo, Jase," called Rand loudly. "You'd better watch where you're going. It's impolite to bump into ladies." The way he said "ladies" was nasty, and Judy heard the insult. She flushed more deeply and put her head in her good hand and just sat.

I felt so awful!

"Come on, Judy," I said. "Let me help."

I started gathering her things and mine. Somebody snickered when I picked up her pocketbook. "Looks cute, Jase." Others giggled, too.

Judy flinched like she'd been hit.

"They weren't laughing at you," I said. "They were laughing at me."

I doubted that she even heard me, let alone believed me.

Mrs. Stevens appeared and got down beside Judy. She began talking softly to her. Mr. Freneau, the science teacher, dispersed the crowd. Soon only Judy, Mrs. Stevens, and I were left.

"Judy, all your things are here," I said to the top of her head. She gave no indication of hearing.

"Rand pushed me, Judy," I said. I wanted her to understand that I hadn't knocked into her on purpose. "I wasn't looking where I was going and I bumped into him and he pushed me and I bumped you. I'm sorry!"

Judy didn't respond.

Mrs. Stevens looked at me and smiled sadly. "You go on to class, Jase. Thanks for your help."

The rest of the day dragged. I could hardly concentrate on my work. At the end of English class, my last class of the day, Mrs. Stevens asked me to stay for a minute. "Tell me what happened in the hall," she said.

I explained to her about Derek and the peanut and Rand and Judy. Mrs. Stevens nodded.

"Is she all right?" I asked.

Mrs. Stevens shrugged. "I wanted her to go home because she was so upset, but she wouldn't. She said she had something too important to do this afternoon to go home. I took her to the nurse's office then, and she was resting there."

"She wants to see the list of those who made cheerleader," I said.

Mrs. Stevens looked concerned. "She tried out?"

I nodded.

By the time I left Mrs. Stevens's room, the halls were empty. I walked slowly toward the gym. I passed a bulletin board where ISN'T HE GRAND was placed squarely on top of JASE SET THE PACE. Three guesses who did that. I realigned the posters so everybody was showing evenly.

Just as I pushed in the last thumbtack, I heard someone scream, "Help me! Someone, help me!"

As many times as I'd heard people yell that on TV, I couldn't believe I was actually hearing it in real life.

"Help! Please, somebody! Help me!"

It was Mary Ellen!

14

I raced down the hall, trying to figure out where the screams were coming from. Suddenly Mary Ellen burst out of the girls' bathroom. Her face was white and her eyes were wide with fear.

"Jase!" She grabbed my arm and pulled. "Help me!"

"What's wrong?"

"It's Judy. Something's wrong with her! Come on!"

I pulled back at the bathroom door. "I can't go in there?"

"Yes, you can! You have to!"

I flinched at the thought of what the guys would say, especially Rand, if they ever found out that I went into the girls' bathroom, but I let Mary Ellen pull me in. She seemed so upset that I didn't know what else to do.

"What should we do?" she said, pointing to Judy.

Judy was lying on the floor, half under the door of one of the stalls. She was unconscious and a pasty white color.

"Is she alive?" I asked. I started coughing this little cough because all the saliva in my mouth suddenly dried up.

"I don't know," said Mary Ellen. "I'm afraid to touch her."

"What happened to her?" I asked, getting down on one knee for a close look.

"I don't know." Mary Ellen was trembling. "I was washing my hands, and I thought I was alone. All of a sudden, Judy just tumbled to the floor and lay there." Mary Ellen gave a great shiver and said simply, "She scared me."

"I bet she did." She scared me, too. I reached out and touched Judy's hand. It was warm and unresponsive. "Did you ever take anybody's pulse before?" I asked.

Mary Ellen shook her head, "Only my dolls when I was little. I just know you shouldn't use your thumb."

"Why not?"

"I don't know."

Big help.

I put my fingers on Judy's wrist. I felt nothing, so I moved them around a little.

"I think I feel something," I said. I leaned real close

to her face and put my cheek next to her mouth. "I think I can feel her breathe, too." I sat back. "We've got to get help!"

"I'll go!" and with that Mary Ellen was gone, leaving me alone in the girls' bathroom with an unconscious girl. The school office was all the way at the far end of the building. If there was still someone in the office, how long would it take her to get them here?

I looked at Judy. I felt like I should do something, but I had no idea what. Should I give her water? They did that in the old cowboy movies. Should I move her? Did she have seizures or something regularly? What was a stroke like? Could kids have heart attacks?

I looked around. Judy's purse had fallen when she had, and the stuff in it lay all over the floor. I gathered it up and stuffed it back in for the second time today, the dirty brush, the cracked mirror, the novel, the used tissues.

I was zipping her bag shut when a terrible thought hit me. I pulled the bag open again and dumped everything back onto the floor.

It wasn't there!

I got down my my knees and looked all over, under the sink, behind the toilets. It wasn't there. I grabbed the wastebasket and dumped it on the floor. Millions of paper towels tumbled out, all crunched up, some still wet, some smeared with enough lipstick that I figured Heidi must have been here earlier.

"It's got to be here," I mumbled. "It's got to be!"

I began shoving the towels back in the wastebasket one at a time until finally I heard the little click of a plastic bottle hitting the floor. I grabbed the bottle and shook it; it was silent. I pulled off the cap and stared in; it was empty.

"Judy!" I yelled. "You took all this medicine!"

I looked at the bottle more closely. Her mom's name was on it.

"Judy, you idiot!" I yelled again. "This was your mother's medicine!" She didn't respond. I grabbed her wrist again but by now I was too upset to find the pulse.

God, don't let her die! Please! Let it be that I'm too dumb to find her heartbeat, not that it's gone!

I sat on the floor beside her and held her hand because I didn't know what else to do. Every so often I said, "Judy, don't die. Please. God, don't let her die. Please."

It was a great relief to me when Mrs. Bartlett, the school nurse, and Mr. Esperanza, the principal, burst into the room with Mary Ellen right behind them. Mrs. Stevens followed to see what all the excitement was about.

Mrs. Bartlett immediately took Judy's pulse and sighed with relief.

"I think she took her mother's pills," I said to Mr. Esperanza. "At least I know this bottle was almost full earlier today, and it's empty now. I found it in the wastebasket."

He took the bottle and handed it to Mrs. Bartlett. She looked at it sadly and shook her head.

I looked at Mary Ellen. What did that head shake mean? That there was no hope? Or was she just distressed?

Mrs. Bartlett and Mr. Esperanza laid Judy flat on the floor.

"The paramedics are on the way but in the meantime, a cold, wet cloth, Cheech," Mrs. Barlett said to Mr. Esperanza.

He pulled a couple of paper towels from the dispenser and held them under the cold water tap. He wrung them out and folded them and handed them to Mrs. Bartlett. She wiped Judy's face and put them on her forehead.

When the cold water first hit her face, Judy sort of shivered and tried to pull her face away. She didn't wake up though.

Mary Ellen and I watched from the doorway with Mrs. Stevens, and I for one felt more hopeful with that slight movement.

Mrs. Kyroni appeared and began crying when she saw Judy.

"It's not your fault," said Mrs. Stevens to her over and over. "It's not your fault."

"I knew cheering meant more to her than it should," said Mrs. Kyroni. "But I didn't know she'd try something like this!"

An ambulance appeared, lights flashing. Two men and a woman rushed into the girls' bathroom. Quickly they replaced Mrs. Bartlett and Mr. Esperanza in caring for Judy. They established for themselves that she was still breathing, and they put an I.V. in her arm, attaching the tube to a bag of clear liquid. They talked to the hospital on a portable phone in what sounded like code. I was in a live *Emergency* rerun!

Mr. Esperanza handed the pill bottle to the lady paramedic.

'How do you know she took these?" the woman asked me.

"I don't. I just know that the bottle was full at lunchtime, that it's empty now, and that I found it in the wastebasket.

Very quickly Judy was placed on a wheeled bed and rolled to the ambulance. They put her in and climbed in after her. In moments they were gone.

"Will she be all right?" Mary Ellen asked Mrs. Bartlett as we watched the blinking lights disappear.

"I don't know for certain," she said, "but I think so."

"What happened, Mary Ellen?" asked Mr. Esperanza.

"I was just washing my hands when all of a sudden she fell on the floor." Mary Ellen shivered again and again, like she couldn't stop. Mrs. Bartlett put her arm around her. "She must have been hiding in one of the stalls."

Mrs. Bartlett nodded. "I've heard of that before. The person swallows the medication, then hides until it takes effect. Then she loses her balance and falls."

"Why would she try to kill herself over cheering?" asked Mrs. Kyroni. She was shaking all over, too.

"It wasn't just cheerleading, Mrs. Kyroni," I said. "Judy had a hard time with lots of things. Nothing seemed to go right for her, and she would get real upset. She's got this really pretty mother and this important father and this cool brother, and she thinks she's awful. She doesn't have any friends, and she wanders around looking lost all the time. Practically no one would sign her petition to be Mayor for a Day, and hardly anyone would come to her party."

"And today she got knocked down in the hall and thought everybody was laughing at her," said Mary Ellen. "And then she didn't make cheerleading. I bet she's already decided that if she couldn't do well enough to make junior high cheerleader, she could never make flag captain for the Royal Raiders, which is a dream of hers."

I nodded. I felt compelled to confess, "I used to think the only thing she had going for her was her brains until last weekend when I learned she could be fun. But Mary Ellen's right. She has lots of problems."

Mrs. Kyroni didn't look quite so upset, and all the others nodded like they understood.

"We want to thank you two for your quick help," said Mr. Esperanza, "Mary Ellen for running to the office so quickly and Jase for finding the empty pill bottle. You two are genuine heroes."

I didn't tell him that I was really just a kid who

108

had never been so scared in his life.

"Now Judy's going to need your help in two more areas," Mr. Esperanza continued. "First, she needs you *not* to tell people about today."

I blinked. I'd already been thinking what a great story this would make.

He looked at us very seriously. "When she wakes up and realizes what she's done, she's going to be very upset, especially when she sees all the people she's hurt and hurt very badly."

I thought of Mrs. Post crying with her beautiful face all sad and Greg being really upset, and I knew Mr. Post wouldn't be taking videos of this performance.

"She'll also learn that the six of us know and be embarrassed by that fact," said Mr. Esperanza. "It becomes very important that Judy knows we're not talking about this with other people. Some of the kids will hear no matter what we do, but if none of us talks about it, the news will be fairly well contained. You two can tell your parents. In fact, I want you to talk with your parents about this. But, please, don't talk to other kids about it. Please."

We nodded. Now that Mr. Esperanza had said it, I could see how upsetting it would be if Judy thought the whole school knew about the overdose.

"The second thing I want you two to do is befriend her," Mr. Esperanza said. "We teachers can only do a small amount. You two can do quite a bit, and I ask you to do all you can."

109

We nodded again, though I couldn't think of anything I could do to help Judy. Hopefully, Mary Ellen had a better imagination than I, though she didn't look very inspired at the moment.

Mr. Esperanza's secretary came hurrying down the hall, a frown on her face. She whispered a message to him while he listened with closed eyes. I think he was as afraid of what she had to say as I was. Then he smiled in relief and said, "Judy will be all right. They pumped her stomach and gave her the proper treatment. One reason they could act so fast was because they had the pill bottle."

Everyone looked at me and smiled. I smiled back.

"I tell you," I said to Mom and Dad later that evening. "I never felt so relieved in all my life."

"I can imagine!" said Mom.

We were all quiet, each thinking about Judy for a few minutes.

"I thought of one thing that I never thought about before," I said. "I've heard about kids committing suicide before and seen stuff about it on TV, but I never realized that suicide is kind of selfish. Judy was trying to take care of her problems in a way she thought would help her, but it would have hurt everybody else, especially her family."

"I can tell you, Jase, that they would never have gotten over it. And I mean never." Mom looked especially sad. "My friend Robin killed herself when we were in high school. Her mother blames herself and is still hurting after all these years."

Once again we sat quietly.

Finally, Dad spoke. "You know, it's sad that some people never learn to give their problems over to God, instead of trying to handle them on their own. He doesn't promise to take away all the bad things that come our way, but at least He is there to share our anxiety and pain."

"A couple of months ago," I said, "Pastor Tony was telling us something like that. He told us that things don't always go right, but it doesn't mean that God's not there. What matters, he said, is what *we* do when things don't go right."

"It's our attitude. . . ." Mom said.

"And our actions. . . ." Dad added.

"That really count," Mom concluded.

"We all have problems," I said, "but you can't kill yourself like Judy tried to do. And you can't go around being a jerk to cover up your problems, like Rand."

Mom and Dad grinned. They love it when I reach good conclusions. They looked like those little dolls whose heads wiggle back and forth forever.

"You know who does the best with his problems?" I asked.

Now their heads went sideways instead of back and forth.

"Mike," I said. "Old Mike. Since he decided to trust Jesus as his Savior, he's tried his best to do what's right no matter what. He still gets hurt by his mom and dad, but he keeps trying to love them anyway. He gets mad, but he tries not to get all moody and upset. He keeps saying, 'I know the Lord is with me. He'll take care of me.' "

Mom and Dad looked at each other, and then turned to look at me. I knew they were proud of me for making such a wise observation.

"I want to be like Mike."

15

I waited in line for my turn to vote. My palms were sweaty and I had that little nervous cough I'd gotten when Judy hurt herself. Did the President feel this way on Election Day?

Mr. Andretti had set up our election very properly. When we came into the gym, we had to give our names and get checked off a list. Then we had to sign our names and we were given a voting form that had Mary Ellen's name, Rand's name, and my name printed on it. We took this form into a little booth and marked our choice for the candidate we wanted. The little booths weren't like the big voting machines I'd seen on TV. They were more like high desks with a shield around three sides and a curtain on the fourth so no one could see in. When we came out, our form was put into a big metal box that had a padlock on it. They would be counted later by Mr. Andretti and Mr. Esperanza.

I marked and folded my ballot and stuffed it into the box. Mike, Jeremy, and Fonz were right behind me. It was comforting to know that at least I'd have three votes besides my own.

Even after I'd voted, I felt like I had a crowd of clowns in my stomach, all of them doing somersaults. In fact, I felt a lot like I had last night when Mom and Dad had taken me to the hospital to visit Judy.

"I don't want to go," I told Mom when she told me Mrs. Post had called and asked if I would come. I took three steps backwards. "Don't make me." I took three more steps backwards and bumped into the wall. I felt cornered. I'd never visited anyone in the hospital before, and the idea scared me, I think, because I didn't know what to expect. Would there be lots of tubes and machines and oxygen and nurses and doctors?

"I don't blame you, Jase," Mom said. "But how can you not go? And we'll go with you. I know you'll make out fine."

There she was, knowing things again.

We took a bunch of balloons with us to give to Judy. They said things like "get well" and "we love you" and were bright colors to cheer her up.

Judy was sitting up in bed watching TV without a tube or machine in sight. She had on a pink bath-

114

robe and her hair was held back with a pink ribbon. Her mother and father were sitting in chairs beside the bed, and Greg was sitting on the foot of the bed trying to do homework. He wasn't being very successful because the rest of the family kept laughing at the TV show.

I was surprised they were laughing. But I was glad. I thought maybe they'd be sitting around crying.

"Jase!" said Mrs. Post when she saw us. "Hal and Ellie, thanks for coming and bringing him."

Mr. Post, whom I'd never met before, stood up and offered Mom his seat. He was a tall man with a big mustache. Both he and Mrs. Post looked tired with big, dark circles under their eyes. I wondered if they had slept at all last night.

"How are you feeling, Judy?" asked Mom.

I was glad she was talking because I didn't know what I should say. Should I talk about yesterday? Should I tell Judy I was glad she was all right? Or should I make believe nothing had happened?

"I'm okay," she said. She clicked off the TV show. "I feel very stupid about what I did, but I'm okay."

"Jase," said Mr. Post, "we want to thank you for what you did yesterday to help Judy. You were there when she needed a friend, and we are in your debt."

"When I think how close we came to losing our baby. . . ." Mrs. Post's voice died away and her eyes filled with tears. She clutched Judy's hand.

At that moment Mary Ellen and Mr. and Mrs. Lafferty walked into the room. In her hand Mary Ellen had a bunch of balloons very much like those I was still holding.

"Man, Judy," said Greg. "It looks like a party in here. Next time you want balloons, just tell me."

Everyone became very busy figuring out where to put the balloons. One set finally got tied to the crank at the foot of Judy's bed and the other to the handle of her night table drawer.

"Thanks," Judy said. "For the balloons and for helping me."

"I just want you to tell me one thing," I blurted out. "Tell me you're never going to do something like that again."

Now Judy's eyes got all teary. "I won't," she whispered. She cleared her throat. "I can't believe I actually did something so terrible."

"Mr. Esperanza and Mrs. Barlett stopped in this afternoon to see Judy," said her mother. "And Mrs. Kyroni came, too."

"And guess what, Mary Ellen?" Judy asked, all excited. Her cheeks got almost as pink as her bathrobe. "She asked me if I'd help her organize a flag line. Just a small one, she said, with navy and white flags for Keystone."

"With the flags half white and half navy?" asked Mary Ellen.

"On the diagonal, don't you think?" said Judy.

"That's great, Judy," Mary Ellen said. "I know that you'd do a good job getting that set up."

Judy blushed, but I knew that the compliment

from Mary Ellen really made her feel good.

When we all got ready to leave, Mary Ellen said, "Judy, in a couple of weeks a bunch of us are going to the shore for the day with the church youth group. I'm going and Sally and Tobi Jo and Jase and some of the guys. Will you come with us?"

"Oh, I-I-I don't know," Judy said hesitantly.

"Ah, come on, Judy," I said. "You'll have a great time . . . and besides, you need something to think about while you're recuperating, something other than this hospital. How long do you have to stay here? This place gives me the creeps."

"The doctor said that Judy can probably go home tomorrow," Mrs. Post said. "And we'll be glad that she is home with us, and we can put all of this behind us."

On the way home I said, "Wouldn't it have been a lot easier on everybody if Judy'd just asked Mrs. Kyroni about a flag line?"

"Sure," said Dad. "Anything's better than trying what Judy did. But thinking up ways around disappointments is often very hard."

"If she was going to be at school tomorrow, I wonder who she'd have voted for—Mary Ellen or me?"

"Why, you, dear," said Mom. "I know she'd have voted for you. The whole seventh grade is going to vote for you. And I'm so glad Mary Ellen asked her to go with you all to the shore. I just know she'll be fine with all you kids caring for her."

Great, I thought. Baby-sitter for life.

I had cast my vote and was leaving the gym when Rand came in with a bunch of his buddies.

"Too bad you're going to lose, McCarver," yelled one guy, the big, dumb one named Preston.

"Who knows?" I called back, trying to act like I was relaxed.

The day dragged on. Since we had all voted in the morning, we knew Mr. Andretti wanted to announce the winner by the end of the school day. I was in English again when he sent for Mary Ellen and me.

Rand arrived at the same time we did, and we took seats in front of Mr. Andretti's desk. I looked at Rand out of the corner of my eye. I wanted to beat him so badly!

"It was a good campaign and election," Mr. Andretti said. "You all can be proud of yourselves, and I'm sorry you all can't be Mayor for a Day."

He smiled at us and we smiled back. *Get on with it*, I wanted to scream.

"Two of you came within three votes of each other for second and third place. Because of the closeness of the finish, I've decided not to tell you who got what. I think it will be enough to know that the Mayor for a Day for this year is Mary Ellen Lafferty."

16

"Come on, Jase! I know you can do it!"

My mother's voice echoed all over the stands at the Brandywine Invitational. I shut my eyes and made believe I didn't hear her. After all, she had known I would win the election, too, and I hadn't.

I still tingled when I remembered Mr. Andretti's announcement yesterday. It had been bad enough when he had made it to just Rand, Mary Ellen, and me, but when he had made it over the school's public address system, it had been awful.

Everybody in our room had clapped for Mary Ellen, including me, of course. But I felt so funny inside. I guess Judy must have felt the same way—only worse—when she read the cheerleaders' list.

"Losing is as much a part of life as winning," Dad said at dinner. "It's just not so much fun."

"Tell me about it," I was having a hard time not sulking. It was interesting that two days after I made my little speech about reacting to bad times in a right way, I had my opportunity to practice what I preached. And I owed it all to the girls of the seventh grade at Keystone Junior High School. They had probably all voted for Mary Ellen, Mr. Andretti said.

The guys had probably split almost evenly between Rand and me. I found it sad that half the guys in my class were dumb enough to vote for Rand.

But if I was having a hard time, Rand was beside himself. He was grumpy and critical and mocking, and he took most of it out on me.

"Back off, Rand," I told him at one point during the warm-ups this morning. He'd just finished singing his version of "The Farmer in the Dell:"

"Little Jase is kind of short.
Little Jase is kind of dumb.
Ho ho, what does he know
He thinks that he can run."

"I heard once that some people feel good when they can make another person feel bad," said Jeremy. "So don't feel bad, and he won't feel good."

"Sounds fine, Jeremy," I said, nodding my head. "I'll try not to get upset that this hulk is mocking me and making my life miserable."

"That's the spirit!" Jeremy said with confidence. He was happy. He'd found the solution to my problem. The trouble was that it didn't work that simply.

I was learning how much I needed to talk to God if I was going to do things right. It wasn't too great to realize that I would rather sulk, be nasty, and complain than act decently. And I didn't want to be a phony, making believe I was wonderful when inside I was a jerk.

"Rand, pay attention to present business," said Mr. Andretti. "We are a team, and we will not criticize others."

"Okay, Mr. Andretti," Rand said, all smiles. As he turned to take the place Mr. Andretti indicated to him, he looked at me and snarled.

Suddenly the dumbness of the whole thing hit me, and I smiled.

Rand jerked like I'd hit him, so I smiled harder.

The Invitational was only relays, no individual races or field events, but it was still an all-day affair. Mr. Andretti only brought sixteen of us, two 400-meter teams and two 800-meter teams. Mike, who had gotten to the point where he actually felt affection for the team, had come with my family.

We had to run qualifying heats before we ever got near the races that counted. So that the most kids could participate, Mr. Andretti only let us run in one event. Mine was to be the 800-meter (100 pounds and under).

While teams waited for their turns, they sat around in bunches on the grass. They played cards and backgammon and two guys even played chess all day.

Some kids had brought their earphones and lay around listening to music, occasionally singing a line of a song and sounding a lot like sheep bleating. Derek had brought along a sports trivia game that we played on and off all day.

My relay team did very well in the qualifying heats and we ended up with the third best time going into the finals. Fonz's 400-meter team got knocked out in their first qualifier, but he didn't seem to care. He was whipping everybody in sports trivia.

Rand's relay team, 800 meters (100 pounds and over), made it to the finals with the second best time.

Our team lined up with the five others for the final race. I checked Jeremy out carefully to make certain he wasn't wearing his sweats. He and Gary and Warren were at the proper places and wearing the proper clothes.

"On your mark!" yelled the starter. "Get set!"

The pistol fired and I was off. After yesterday's loss, I was hungry for a win today. I gave it everything I had, and we were slightly ahead when I handed off to Jeremy in a perfect pass that must have made Mr. Zindorf very happy.

Jeremy was in good form, too. He sailed along, his feet barely touching the ground. His pass to Gary was a thing of beauty.

I could hear my mom. "Come on, Keystone. I know you can do it."

"Come on, Gary!" I screamed. "You can do it! I know you can do it!"

One trouble with running the relay is that your success depends on the performance of others. All you can do is stand on the sidelines and cheer.

The other problem, by far the worse of the two, is that while you're waiting for the rest of the race, you start cheering just like your mother.

"Come on, guys!" I yelled. "I know you can do it!"

Gary passed to Warren cleanly, and he began the final leg of the race about two steps behind this guy from Fromley, a track powerhouse of a school district.

"Go, Warren!" I screamed. "Go! You can do it!"

And he did! He and the Fromley guy were stride for stride for a short time, and then Warren got an extra burst from somewhere. He hit the tape about two steps ahead of the Fromley guy.

We all jumped up and down and screamed and yelled like idiots. It was great fun.

"New question for the sports trivia game!" screamed Fonz as he jumped. "Who were the members of the famous Keystone 800-meter relay squad (100 pounds and under)? Answer: McCarver, Barnes, Goerlich, and Jones!" he yelled, and we all cheered.

"Sounds like a dopey law firm to me," said Rand. I guess that if it was sometimes hard for me to be happy when Rand won, it was harder still for him to be pleased when I won.

When Rand's relay team took to the field, I was still feeling so good that I cheered and screamed as if Rand were a best buddy. When he came thundering down the last stretch full out for the finish line, I yelled for him as loudly as all the other guys did. When he and his team took first, I jumped up and down as happily as they did. Because of the two firsts, Keystone was the day's winning team. A happy Mr. Andretti was rubbing his hands so hard I was afraid he'd rub his skin right off.

Mom, Dad, Matty, and Mike joined us at the end of the meet. Rand and I were allowed to ride home with them instead of on the school van.

Matty especially was bubbling with excitement.

"That was great, Jase," he kept saying over and over. "That was great!"

He went up to Rand and said, "That was great, Rand! Just great!"

Rand actually smiled and said, "Thanks, kid."

Instead of stopping while he was ahead, Matty kept on talking.

"I'm sorry you lost the election yesterday," he said.

"And you're not sorry Jase lost?"

"Of course I'm sorry Jase lost," said Matty. "He's my brother."

"But we both couldn't have won," said Rand.

"But one of you could, and then the guys would have beaten the girls." Matty grinned. "I like to beat the girls. The girls are the enemy, you know."

Rand smiled for a second time. "You won't talk that way for much longer," he said. "Soon you'll think they're wonderful."

"So I hear," said Matty. "But I don't believe it. What

we should have done was make you and Jase more posters and signs and badges and stuff. Then one of you might have won."

I would have strangled the kid if I could have reached him in time, but I couldn't. Rand was staring strangely at him, a bewildered look on his face.

"What did you say?" Rand asked.

"We should have made more posters and stuff."

"You made my posters?" Rand sounded like he was talking underwater. The words sort of gurgled out.

Matty nodded happily. "Didn't Jase tell you? He even made one, the STRIKE UP THE BAND one."

I looked at Mom and Dad and Mike. Mom and Dad were listening with interest. They wanted to see Rand's reaction. Mike was listening with a funny smile on his face. He edged over to me.

"I thought your family probably did those posters, but did you actually make that big one yourself?"

"In a weak moment," I said. "And I've regretted it many times since."

All the way home, Rand didn't say a word. The rest of us talked nonstop, but Rand just sat. Every so often, he touched the gold medal hanging around his neck, but that was it. I understood that; I kept touching mine, too.

When we got to his house, Rand climbed out of the backseat he had shared with Mike and me. He leaned down and looked in at my parents.

"Thanks for the ride," he said. "See you later, Matty."

He turned to go.

Mike and I looked at each other and nodded.

"See you later, Rand," I called.

"So long, Rand," called Mike.

We grinned at each other.

Rand turned back and looked at me with a funny expression.

"McCarver," he said, "you drive me crazy."

7TH GRADE SOCCER STAR

Jason made the team, but. . .

Jason McCarver knew the competition would be tough when he saw how many guys turned out for the seventh grade soccer team. But, he hadn't counted on Rand Purcell. He was big, he was good, and he seemed to delight in making life miserable for Jason.

Then there was the other problem—the fact that Jason was adopted and never felt like he fit in. Why did his birth mother give him up for adoption? Was he really a "reject"? And, would God be able to help him with his problems?

Be sure to read other White Horse boys sport stories:

A Winning Season for the Braves
Mystery Rider at Thunder Ridge
At Left Linebacker, Chip Demory
Batter Up!
Full Court Press
A Race to the Finish

GAYLE ROPER, accomplished author and seminar speaker, lives in Coatesville, PA. She is the mother of two adopted sons.

Chariot Books™
David C. Cook Publishing Co.

55079   ISBN 1-55513-507-2